CW01500860

ACKNOWLEDGMENTS

Thank you to my first readers: Dawn Simpson, Brenda Hill, and Sue Billings for your comments and suggestions. Also, a big thank you goes out to Linda LaRoque and Sue Billings for your editing expertise.

LINE DANCING CAN BE MURDER

BY

STACEY COVERSTONE

DEDICATION

To my lifelong friends: Dawn, Linda, Susan, Sallie, Brenda and Sheryl—ladies who love to line dance together, but have never murdered anyone, as far as I know.

CHAPTER ONE
Teresa

It was my suggestion for the six of us to go on a bus tour to celebrate Annette's birthday. She was going to be the first in our group to hit the big five-o, with the rest of us following close on her heels.

Every Monday night for the past couple of years, in between the country songs we line danced to in Crystal's garage, I listened to my lifelong friends complain about their aches and pains, tiresome careers, disappointments regarding children and men, and the general dissatisfaction with getting older. That particular night, the whining seemed to hit an all-time high.

The weather didn't help. It was January, which meant bundling in layers to go anywhere and trying not to go crazy listening to wind that screeched like a witch. It was so bone-chilling cold, the snow that had fallen two weeks earlier in our small town of Harley's Grove, Illinois hadn't yet melted. The miserable weather was enough to make a soul go into hibernation until spring. Adding to the black mood, all of us except Jackie had gained a couple of pounds over the holidays.

Never one for pity, self or otherwise, the light

bulb moment flashed in my brain while dancing to Trace Adkins' *Honky Tonk Badonkadonk*. After the song ended, I gasped for oxygen and reached for my water bottle. "Hey, girls, I think we should start off our year of birthdays in grand fashion. An acquaintance recently told me about a bus tour out west she took last June. She said it was the best time she's ever had. Let's pick a date that works for us all this summer and go! We need to get out of Mayberry and do something special for ourselves. Who's with me?"

Crystal's eyebrow arched with interest. Jackie rolled her eyes and asked why a bus? Annette liked the idea. She said it would do her good to get away from the office for a week, as well as her husband and son. Kim said "no" immediately. She worries that her live-in boyfriend might find another woman if she's out of his sight for one minute. Donna, who became widowed only a year and a half ago, smiled and said she had a little nest egg she could tap into. Her husband didn't enjoy traveling, but she always wanted to.

It didn't take much persuasion for the four of us eager for adventure to convince the other two who were initially opposed. That's how the nine-day National Parks Wonders Tour plan came into being. We booked it for June during the same week as Annette's birthday.

The decision lifted our spirits and helped us get through the rest of the depressing Midwest winter. We had something to look forward to besides turning another year older and dealing with life's daily grinds. But I'll admit, if I'd known I'd be coming home from that trip a murderess, I probably would have thought twice about going.

That's right, I said murder.

To look at me, you wouldn't guess me to be the homicidal type. My hair, which Kim dyes red to hide the gray, is naturally curly and frizzes like crazy on humid days. I wear glasses when I read or work on the computer. I'm slim but can easily put on weight when I give in to my obsession with sweets. I enjoy clothes and dress fashionably. On a scale from one to ten, I give myself a 7.5 in looks.

I grew up in Harley's Grove, a happy and well-adjusted child with two parents who adored each other. They showered me with love and self-confidence, and although we were middle class, my every need was provided for. I won numerous awards in school, including one for being a good citizen, a band camp scholarship, and the Daughters of the American Revolution Award.

In other words, I'm a pretty normal person.

The local American Legion selected me as the Girl's State representative during my junior year of high school. My reward for that honor was wasting a week of my summer vacation at Southern Illinois University. Girls from all over the state gathered to participate in mock government activities. I didn't understand how government functioned then, and I still don't care two hoots for politics. The best part of the experience was that I immediately clicked with my roommate, a Jewish girl from a Chicago suburb who was obsessed with sex, drugs, and European men, which made her seem very worldly, if not a little slutty. Somehow she'd managed to smuggle in some pot without the dorm mother knowing. Sneaking out at night to smoke with her made the week tolerable.

As an adult, I've made some mistakes (who hasn't?), but for the most part I've behaved as a model citizen within my community. My grownup life has been relatively uneventful and lacking in stress (up until I murdered someone, that is). I attribute my carefree existence to having had no children and never being married. That's not to say I haven't been in love. I have.

Engaged twice in my younger years, it was my choice to break off the relationships both times. And before you ask, no, I'm not a closet lesbian or a-sexual or repressed or frigid. In fact, having sex is still as important to me as breathing air and as satisfying as eating chocolate.

My father pegged it, however, when he'd proudly tell people that I was too headstrong, outspoken and independent to put up with a man for an entire lifetime. I always agreed with him. But it's not as if my expectations for a relationship were so high, especially in the beginning. With all that testosterone oozing from their pores, males are simply their own worst enemy. With Dad as the exception, the majority of guys I dated or was intimate with started out decent and then quickly morphed into dogs, pigs, or pig-dogs with monkey brains.

So I've made a life for myself. I don't have complaints, because my choices have been my own. One of them was quitting college to find myself. Finding myself took quite a long time, and once I finally succeeded, myself had no interest in furthering my education. Therefore, I have no degree hanging on my office wall. What I do have is a certificate stating I was Employee of the Month in October 2002. That was the one and only time management gave out such an award. I'm not sure what that says about management, or my coworkers.

My job as Office Manager and Bookkeeper for the trucking company outside of town hasn't been a thrill a minute, but it's provided me with stability, freedom, and a good retirement plan. I drive a nice car, and I own my home, a three-bedroom rancher surrounded by oak trees in the same neighborhood where I was raised.

As for my love life… Occasionally, Phil, a butcher at the IGA who could pass for Sam Elliott at a distance, will park his truck in the alley behind my house. He'll bring two steaks or a package of pork chops beautifully cut and wrapped in clean white paper. He'll feed me and then stay the night. Phil works out. For a man closing in on sixty, his muscles are also cut beautifully.

Our trysts have been going on for about eight months. Though Harley's Grove is a small town and gossip travels fast, people don't seem to talk about us. We don't give them reason to. The only time we're together outside of my bedroom is when he takes me target shooting in the woods.

I'm good with guns. Shooting is serious business, but afterwards, we laugh and Phil will cup my bottom in his big hand and tell me I'm like no other woman he's known. I just smile and remind him of our agreement: No strings attached, no promises for the future, and no using the "L" word. Most of the time he smiles back, but there are moments when his big mustache will droop under a frown. I feel bad when he looks at me that way. But I decided a long time ago that I would live life on my own terms, and no man would ever change me.

My entire existence has been spent in my hometown. At this age, I couldn't imagine living anywhere else. It's comfortable here. I know every sidewalk and street so well, I could walk anywhere with my eyes closed and not get run down by a car or fall off a curb or bump into a trash can.

Life is full. I enjoy throwing casual dinner parties, going to the movies, and working in the garden in the spring and summer. In the winter, I catch up on reading and stay active by line dancing. The exercise keeps me in shape. More than that, it's a way to stay connected to my good friends—the ladies I consider my sisters: Jackie, Crystal, Annette, Kim, and Donna.

Friends since childhood, we know each other better than we know our own family members. Growing up in our town, there wasn't much for teenagers to do on Friday and Saturday nights except to hang out, gossip, and cruise Main Street scouting for members of the opposite sex. The hope was to find Mr. Right, or at least Mr. Right for Tonight. That was the seventies. The AIDS crisis hadn't yet come onto the scene, and we were just looking for a fun time.

In this year of 2013, things haven't changed much. Harley's Grove has decreased in population by more than half, and most of the small businesses have closed down. Most people now work and shop in the university town thirty minutes away. Although kids still just want to have fun, Main Street cruising is a thing of the past. But that doesn't mean the hunt for the right man has stopped.

A few of my girlfriends are still looking and

hoping for a miracle in that department. But guys have a way of screwing things up big time, unless the woman controls the situation. I learned that ages ago as well. Unfortunately, before we took our trip together, some of my gal pals were still in need of learning that lesson. I became their teacher.

Actually, we were just kids when I naturally gravitated toward being the ringleader of our little circus. When one of us was mad at the other, I acted as peacemaker. If one of us was in trouble, I rounded up the troops and figured out how we could help. When group decisions needed to be made, I stepped up and made them.

I'd do anything for my friends. They know that. Which is precisely how I got myself into hot water. Dammit! If they didn't mean so much to me, Keith Creswell wouldn't have had to die that night in South Dakota.

CHAPTER TWO
Jackie

"Can't we forget the rest of the trip and stay here in Vegas? I like this hotel with its pool and gambling casino." Wearing round sunglasses, strappy high-heeled sandals, a flowing top with big pink roses across the bosom, and white stretch pants that clung to a figure that could still be considered girlish, Jackie led our gang through the Hilton Hotel lobby to the area where we were to meet up with the tour guide and fellow travelers for a welcome reception. Looking like a super model, she flipped her long ash blond hair over a shoulder and strutted like a peacock, catching the glances of everyone we passed.

"I'm glad we're only staying one night here," Crystal said. She nervously stared at the one-armed bandit machines as we walked by an entire banquet-sized room filled with them. "I've heard people can lose all their money in one night of gambling. That would be terrible to lose everything on the first night of vacation. What would someone do for the other eight days of the tour? There wouldn't be anything left for souvenirs or food."

"Live a little," Jackie snorted. "This is probably your one and only time in Sin City. You've got to try your hand at one game before we leave. You'll regret it if you don't. Who knows? Maybe you'll strike gold."

"Nope." Crystal vigorously shook her head. "Easy for you to take risks with money. You're married to a man richer than God."

It was true. Jackie's fourth husband was one of the wealthiest men in Illinois. He was also one of the oldest. In his eighties with a myriad of health problems, his body was expected to give out any day. When Jackie married him ten months ago, his doctor had given him less than three months to live. She hadn't planned on him surviving this long. Her weekly updates about his stabilized health have become laced with more frustration as the months have drawn on.

The poor man was blind in one eye, had suffered congestive heart failure, and never got out of his wheelchair except to be put into bed. He wore a catheter and oxygen tube. Professional nurses watched him around the clock.

Although Jackie sounded like a bitch when she wondered out loud how long the man could possibly last, deep down inside she wasn't a bad person. She'd treated Milton kindly from day one. In return, he'd married her and was leaving everything to her: his lifetime accumulation of wealth, the mansion, expensive jewelry, and ten vehicles. His first wife had passed away twenty-five years ago and they'd had no children.

Luckily for Jackie, Milton's lawyers had made the changes to his will before dementia completely stole his mind. So far, no secret heirs or extended family members had crept out of the cracks to challenge her or the will. Even if someone disputed the will after Milton's death, no one would have a leg to stand on, she says. She is, after all, his legal wife, and entitled to his inheritance.

Not so long ago, I asked her if she regretted marrying him. To some, the question may have seemed ridiculous. At the time, we were sitting in one of the twenty magnificent rooms of her mansion and sipped tea that was served by a woman in a maid's uniform who'd been several years behind us in school.

"What regrets would I have?" she'd asked, looking genuinely confused.

I slipped another finger sandwich off the tray in front of me and took a bite. "Well, you're a vibrant woman who has always had an active sex life." I rarely minced words. Despite being one of my best friends, Jackie earned a reputation in high school for being an easy girl, and it had stayed with her through the years.

She married the first time shortly after we graduated. Turned out, Tim couldn't wait to get married just so he could demand intercourse whenever he wanted. *Dog.* Although Jackie was quick to admit she liked sex, being forced was another thing altogether. The straw that broke that camel's back a year into the marriage was that he suggested a threesome with a girl he'd met at the local bar. *Pig.* She'd kicked him out and then discovered she was pregnant.

All three men Jackie was married to before Milton had known how to please a woman in bed, she used to brag. Unfortunately, they'd each left her with a child, a pile of unpaid bills, broken dreams, and low self-esteem. In one case, all she got out of the union was a black eye and a broken pinkie finger. *Pig-dogs*.

I suppose that's why she felt entitled to Milton's fortune. She thought she'd gone through enough hell in one lifetime and deserved to live the rest of her years in luxury and comfort.

"Don't you miss having sex?" I asked that day, clarifying my question. "You've been married ten months, but I can't imagine…" I couldn't finish the sentence because I literally couldn't imagine.

Her answer surprised me, although I'm not sure why, knowing Jackie.

"I don't miss sex," she'd said, lighting a slim cigarette that was stuck in a sleek black holder like movie stars used in the fifties. "Do you know Chris Stevens?"

I thought a moment and recalled a kid by that name who had been a freshman when we were seniors. I remembered he'd been a good athlete and had made the varsity football team that year. "Doesn't he work as a carpenter around town?"

She nodded and ran her tongue over her lip. "Yes, he does. And let me tell you, that guy can hammer until the cows come home, if you catch my drift."

I did catch it and groaned at her stupid joke.

Physically shuddering, Jackie smiled, apparently recollecting more of her exploits with Chris. "Teresa, you wouldn't believe the things that man can do with his *tools*." It really hadn't been necessary for her to emphasize the word. I understood. "I'm telling you," she continued, "your life would change if you were to get nailed by a man like that. *Change*," she stressed again.

Rolling my eyes, I stood up and said it was time for me to go. My life was fine, thank you, and no change to it was required. Although I never spoke of Phil, I was pretty sure Jackie knew about him and me, but I guess she didn't consider him any match for Chris Stevens when it came to physical prowess.

I'm far from a prude, but her husband was upstairs crippled, breathing and peeing through tubes. If Milton was going to hand over to her what he'd worked a lifetime to achieve, I felt she should at least wait until he'd kicked the bucket before finding another dog to breed with. Her lack of commitment to her marriage vows ticked me off.

Thank goodness she'd had her tubes tied years ago and was no longer of the age where she could procreate with Chris, or whomever else found their way into her bed. The three children she has barely speak to her. I reminded her that without Milton, she'd still be living in the trailer park. In my mind, *she* owed *him*. And I told her so before striding through the big front door and slamming it hard behind me.

Our little dispute didn't last long. Although I didn't agree with what she was doing, it wasn't my business, and Jackie always has a way of drawing you back to her, like a bee to its hive.

We stopped to window shop at one of the hotel's boutiques.

"That beaded purse is three hundred and fifty dollars!" Kim squawked. "It's so pretty, but Eddie would kill me if I spent that kind of money on a purse. He thinks Walmart has the best prices, and people are stupid for paying more for anything somewhere else."

"Who cares what Eddie thinks," Annette said.

"You're not even married to the man. You own your own beauty shop. Can't you spend your money the way you want?"

Kim's head snapped around. "At least Eddie's at home every night."

I could see the comment stung Annette. Her lips twisted into what my mother would have called an ugly mouth. I eased Kim away from the boutique window and a possible punch in the arm from Annette. "Look! It's Elvis!" I exclaimed.

We all strolled by a large statue of Elvis Presley playing a guitar and then rounded the corner and saw the sign: *NATIONAL PARKS WONDERS TOUR CHECK-IN.* When we entered a small banquet room, it looked like we were the last to arrive. A swarm of people (nearly all were elderly, I noticed immediately) greeted each other shaking hands and introducing themselves. A bald black man with a friendly smile sat behind a table. As we gave him our names, he marked them off a list and handed each of us a nametag.

"Welcome to the National Parks Wonders Tour, ladies. I'm Wayne, and I'll be your bus driver for the trip. Please wear these nametags at least for the first few days, until everyone gets to know each other." He directed our attention to a table laden with soft drinks and cookies. "Help yourselves to refreshments and mingle with your fellow travelers. In a few minutes, your tour director will give a short introduction."

We were so excited to be in Las Vegas and to start this once-in-a-lifetime adventure. Fortunately, the tension between Annette and Kim from moments before disappeared, and all of us tittered like children.

"I think everyone in this room is over sixty-five,"

Annette whispered, as we gazed around.

Kim elbowed Jackie in the rib. "Maybe you'll meet your next husband here."

"Very funny," Jackie deadpanned.

"We're the spring chickens in the group." I noticed two old men across the room waving their hands off. One raised his plastic glass in the air. Both started sauntering toward us.

"Oh, no. Here come Romeo and Casanova," Donna chuckled.

The gentlemen said hello. The one wearing a plaid golf cap was clearly extroverted while the other seemed pretty shy. He wore a Cincinnati Reds baseball cap. They were both in short-sleeved button-up shirts. Jackie, Crystal, Kim and Annette quickly deserted Donna and I, leaving us trapped in a corner by the two septuagenarians.

It wasn't but a few minutes before Wayne pleasantly called the room to order. "Now that everyone is here and checked in, it's time to introduce you to your tour director. Keith, come on out."

A man, whom I now know had been thirty-four at the time, stepped from behind a curtain like a movie star making an entrance. Audible gasps emanated from the women in the room. With a head of blond hair and blue eyes that twinkled (yes, they actually twinkled), a granite jaw, and the body of Adonis, the guy was drop dead gorgeous. Once he opened his mouth, his charm and personality shone immediately. It was obvious he was born for this job. With a bright and confident smile, I deduced, if he hadn't been a tour bus guide, he would have made a great snake oil salesman.

When he locked eyes with me, the hairs on my

arms prickled, and a chill ran through my body. I'd never had a psychic experience before, but the strangest feeling washed over me, as if I could foretell the way things would turn out for him. And, for me.

"Good afternoon, everyone! I'm Keith Creswell. We're going to be spending the next nine days together, and I guarantee, they're going to be nine of the best days and nights of your life." His gaze finally snapped away from me, and he winked at one of the blue-haired ladies.

Everyone clapped and nodded. A few of the women giggled, including Crystal. I glanced at plaid golf cap man. He didn't look pleased. It was my guess he hoped to find his Ms. Right or Ms. Right for Tonight on this trip. How did he stand a chance if Keith, the Greek God, got all the attention?

I held in a chuckle. Despite the weird sensation moments earlier, I felt as happy as a child on Christmas morning. I so looked forward to a vacation with my friends. But my smile turned upside down when I looked at Jackie and saw her staring at Keith and licking her lips.

CHAPTER THREE
Donna

"Enjoy the rest of your day and evening at your leisure," Keith said, finishing his short speech. "Tomorrow morning, breakfast is at the Paradise Café here in the hotel. Bring your luggage to the side entrance anytime after six-thirty. The bus will be in the parking lot. Wayne and I will load and unload your bags every day. Boarding tomorrow starts at seven-thirty and we leave at eight o'clock sharp, so don't be late. Everybody clear?"

"Clear!" the group shouted.

"All right." A hundred-watt grin filled Keith's handsome face. He squeezed the hand of another older woman traveler. "See you all in the morning, bright-eyed and bushy-tailed." He waved as if he were a prince acknowledging his throngs of admirers and disappeared back behind the curtain like one of the magic acts Vegas was known for.

That moment has stuck in my mind ever since. Certainly, I wish things had turned out differently, but what's done is done. Keith had no clue that his freewheeling life would be over in eight short days. And I had no idea I'd be the one to end it.

"Forget Elvis," Crystal said. "There goes a real hunka hunka burnin' love."

Jackie rolled her eyes. "Really, Crystal, stop drooling."

"I noticed you staring pretty hard," Crystal shot back. "I'm single. I'm allowed. You're not."

Understanding Crystal's sensitivity when it came to infidelity, I wanted to change the subject fast before a catfight started. I suggested we choose roommates, check into our rooms, and then decide our plans for the rest of the day.

"I'll room with anyone but Jackie," Crystal said, not looking at her.

"I don't mind bunking with you, girlfriend." Kim bumped hips with Jackie.

Donna looked at me. "Do you want to be my roomie?"

She and I had always been good friends growing up, but we'd become even closer during her husband's illness. From the moment Chad was diagnosed with lung cancer, I'd been there for her as much as possible. The others had done what they could, but I'd had a lot of vacation time saved up that allowed me to help when they couldn't.

When Donna couldn't get off work, I drove Chad to his treatments. I regularly cleaned the house for her, did her grocery shopping, and made meals. Stress and depression had caused her to become mentally and physically exhausted. I was an ear for her when she vented over how unfair life was. Chad had never smoked, which we all thought was a terrible travesty. When he died after a short battle, I was Donna's shoulder to cry on.

I chuckled and linked my arm through hers. "We can room together if you promise not to snore."

"Promise. I brought nasal strips with me."

"That leaves Annette and Crystal as a pair." They smiled at each other, satisfied. "Let's get settled into our rooms and then meet back in the lobby in thirty minutes. Sound good?"

They all agreed.

While I was oohing and ahhing over our pretty room, I noticed Donna seemed a little down. "Tired?" I asked.

She shook her head of chestnut brown corkscrew curls and sunk onto the edge of one of the two beds.

I sat next to her believing I knew what the problem was. "Are you thinking about Chad and wishing he was here with you?"

She smiled but looked on the verge of tears. "He never liked to travel, as you know. He was a home body."

Chad had always been that way. He and I had grown up next door to each other, and his family had never taken a vacation in their lives, as far as I knew. His lack of interest in traveling must have come natural. "Then what is it, Donna?" I was sensitive to her emotions, but dang it, we were supposed to have left our troubles at home and be enjoying the vacation of a lifetime.

"I told you all I had a little nest egg. And I did," she added quickly. "But I spent most of it to come on this trip. When Chad got sick and had to quit working, we got behind in some of our bills. Our savings was wiped out. We were barely making ends meet, so we cashed in our life insurance policies. I would have lost the house if we hadn't. It was irresponsible of me to take this trip, because now I don't have much cushion left. I should have saved the bit I had for a rainy day. But I didn't want to let all of you down, and I wanted to come with you so badly."

I patted her hand. "You've never let anyone down, Donna. But I wish you'd told us. We're always here for each other. As for this trip, I could have loaned you the money. We wouldn't have come without you."

She nodded. "You girls have done so much for me already, but especially you. I couldn't ask you then or now for loans that I might never be able to pay back."

"You could have asked Jackie," I teased. "She's married to a man richer than God." That was our go-to line when any of us stressed about money.

Donna cracked a smile.

"What about the kids? Can they help out if you're in a bind?" Donna and Chad had two adult children, both married and doing well.

"I won't ask them and don't want them to worry. They have their own families and responsibilities. I'll get by. I'm just feeling guilty about spending so much money for my own pleasure." A tear slipped from her eye.

I hugged her, knowing guilt tugged at her. I'd had to delve into my own savings to pay for the trip, but I felt I deserved it. "Chad would want you to do something nice for yourself. You were a good wife to him for close to twenty-eight years. You stuck by him, through better or worse, richer or poorer, in health and in sickness, all the way to the end. You earned this vacation."

After a few moments, she hugged me back. "You're absolutely right. For these nine days, I'm going to put aside my worries about the future and have fun. That's why I'm here."

"That's why we're all here." I saw concern still etched on her face.

"Maybe when we get home, I'll ask for a raise at work," she mused. "I haven't had one in years." Donna was the office secretary for the high school we attended. "Or I'll start playing the lotto and filling out those Publishers Clearing House sweepstakes forms when they come in the mail. Maybe I'll get lucky."

"Your chances might be better with a one-armed bandit downstairs," I said, wishing she had more realistic options for her financial future.

After we'd freshened up, we met the others in the lobby and unanimously decided to walk the strip. We were anxious to view landmarks we'd always heard about and seen on television.

The fountains and water ballet outside the Bellagio were as pretty as I'd expected. We also saw the volcano at the Mirage, Caesars Palace where Celine Dion performs, and the famous Little White Wedding Chapel. Juggling all of our digital cameras, another tourist took our picture together in front of the forty-foot waving neon cowboy. After we checked out the lobby of every fabulous hotel along the strip, we strolled through the Bonanza, the world's largest gift shop, where Jackie insisted on buying us each a tacky souvenir.

"It must be one hundred degrees in the shade," Crystal complained two hours later as we continued to trudge over hot pavement and jostle our way through crowds. My feet and legs hurt from all the walking and knew she must have been suffering. She was forty pounds heavier than me. Perspiration rolled down her cheeks, and her short hair was as damp as if she'd just gotten out of the shower.

"How long is this strip?" Kim asked.

"The brochure I picked up at the hotel says 4.2 miles," Annette answered, thumbing through a crumpled flyer.

"Four miles? Whose brilliant idea was it to walk the whole thing?" Crystal groaned. "I need a cold drink or I'm going to die."

"We don't have to walk any further," I decided, also hot and thirsty. "We've seen about everything. Let's get something to drink and then take the free shuttle back to the hotel. Is that okay with everyone?"

"Yes," they sighed in unison.

"The pool is calling my name," Jackie said. "I bought several new swimsuits for this trip that I'm eager to try out."

After refreshing ourselves with soft drinks from a sidewalk cart, we wearily climbed aboard a shuttle. I was dabbing my damp face with a Kleenex and gazing around for a seat when I heard a male voice shout out.

"Hey girls! There are seats back here. Come sit with us."

I couldn't believe my eyes. Plaid golf cap man and baseball cap man were waving their hands off again. What were the chances? There were three empty bench seats near them that the six of us made a beeline for. Annette and I flopped into the seat in front of the men and then turned around to say hello.

Plaid golf cap man, AKA Romeo, didn't bother to

hide his interest. His open gaze moved from our faces to our bosoms. Although neither Annette nor I wore revealing clothes, we were both in tank tops and must have looked pretty hot and sexy to the old geezer. We were hot, all right. Sweat dripped down my armpits, and my whole body felt like a furnace.

"Funny meeting you here," he said. "We didn't get a chance to tell you our names back at the welcome reception, or find out yours." He pointed to the nametag on his shirt pocket. "I'm Chuck and this is Bill. We're both retired teachers from Cincinnati."

"Nice to meet you fellows. I'm Teresa and this is my friend, Annette." I nodded toward the other girls across the aisle. "And that's Jackie, Kim, Crystal and Donna. We're all from Illinois."

"What brought you ladies on this tour?" Bill asked in a soft voice.

I liked him. He had warm eyes and a sweet smile. As I regarded the two men more closely, their features were so similar I thought they could have been brothers.

"My birthday is this week on Sunday," Annette answered. "We decided to take this tour as a way to celebrate our upcoming year of birthdays. We're lifelong friends, and I'm the first of us to turn fifty."

It surprised me to hear her mention her impending age so casually. After we'd booked the trip, she'd admitted to me that she hated the idea of becoming fifty. She'd been feeling old and unattractive and wasn't buying the saying: fifty is the new forty. Now she was smiling proudly. Maybe talking to spry men in their seventies brought the whole age thing into perspective for her.

"We'll have to let Keith know about your birthday so he can find a cake," Bill said.

"What a nice idea," Annette replied.

Chuck winked. "I'll be the first in line to give you a birthday kiss."

Annette chuckled. "Sorry. I'm a married woman."

Chuck frowned. "Darn. Those things always get in the way."

Just then, someone's cell phone rang, which was apparently a reminder for Kim. I heard her say she should call Eddie. Her face twisted into a grimace as she dug through her purse. "My cell phone's not here! Oh, crap. I hope I haven't lost it."

"You probably left it in the room," Jackie suggested. "I saw it on the bathroom counter when I was brushing my teeth."

Kim snapped her purse shut and chewed her lip. "I hope you're right. If it's gone, I'm going to have to buy a disposable one. There's no way I can be out of contact with Eddie for nine days."

CHAPTER FOUR
Kim

Kim's greatest desire was to be married. She was one of those girls who had dreamed of her wedding since she was a little girl and had every detail planned out, from the color scheme (red and gold) to the flavor of the cake (red velvet) to the flowers (red roses, of course).

Unfortunately, Eddie, the man she'd been living with for ten years had no intention of tying the knot with her. As my mother used to say, why buy the cow when you can get the milk for free?

Everyone seemed to know this about Eddie except Kim. Every birthday, Valentine's Day, and Christmas for the past eight years, she'd worked herself into a frenzy thinking *that* was the day he was going to propose, only to be disappointed over and over again. My heart broke each time she'd show me a deluxe iron or a three-way lamp or the Fruit of the Month membership he'd bought her.

"I do like oranges and grapefruit, but dammit, all I really want is a little black box from Kay Jewelers!" she cried last Christmas, smashing an orange on her kitchen counter.

One time the fool got her a weed whacker for her birthday! He thought it made sense because the house belonged to Kim and she was the one who mowed the grass and kept the hedges trimmed. For years, his excuse for not helping out with the yard work has been a bad back. The day she showed the weed whacker to me in the garage, she heaved the biggest sobs on my shoulder, and I had the maniacal urge to storm inside the house and whack off one of Eddie's appendages.

As a single woman who enjoys outdoor work, I keep my property maintained myself. But Kim works around the clock at the salon. Every weekend, Eddie sits around her house watching whatever sports is on television and ignoring her, except to grunt like a caveman for her to grab him a beer.

"Why do you continue to put up with such poor treatment?" I asked Kim one day. "There are other fish in the sea, you know." With her shiny dark hair and big brown eyes, I could think of a couple of single men in town who would jump at the chance to date her.

"Nobody knows me like Eddie," she said simply.

That may be true. In the past six months, I've begun to suspect I don't know Kim as well as I imagined. It was during our last New Year's Eve party, held at her house, when the revelation hit me big time.

I'd developed a severe headache and needed to leave early. Eddie told me he'd hung our jackets in the extra bedroom closet. Of course, like the oaf he is, he didn't offer to get my coat for me, so I went myself. When I flung open the closet door, a big box dropped over the edge of the shelf and almost knocked me out. When the box hit the floor, it landed on its side and the flaps flew open. The things that tumbled out shocked me at first, and then sent me into a spiral of confusion.

The box was full of CD's, makeup, lip gloss, jewelry (some expensive, some costume), sexy underwear, unopened packs of cigarettes (Kim doesn't smoke), full perfume bottles, and even some common things like an electric toothbrush, disposable razors, candy bars, kitchen utensils, and ballpoint pens.

I'd barely had time to contemplate what it meant when I heard the bedroom door close. "What are you doing with that?" Kim's enlarged eyes met mine.

"Nothing. I was getting my coat and the dang box fell off the shelf and about decapitated me."

She knelt and furiously scooped everything into the box. Then she slammed the flaps down, heaved the box to her hip, lifted it in the air, and shoved it onto the shelf, pushing it back as far as it would go.

"What is all that stuff?" I asked.

I'd never seen a more guilty looking face in my life. But Kim recovered quickly. "You know how my situation with Eddie can sometimes get me down?" she said.

"Yes."

"Well, when he really makes me angry, I feel better after I've had a little retail therapy. That's all. I hide the stuff in here so he doesn't ask questions. He never comes in this room." Her smile was stiff, and she wrenched her hands together so tightly I thought she'd break some bones.

"Oh." Kim's explanation made sense, because I'd probably be bankrupt from revenge shopping if Eddie was my man. But suspicion niggled under my skin. I believed her about as far as I could throw her. My head pounded and I wanted to go home, so despite my sixth sense that she was into something deeper than she would admit, I didn't try forcing the truth from her. I'm not her mother. But I *am* her friend, and friends have each other's back. No matter how I've tried since then, I can't seem to get that stupid box off my mind.

"Where'd you get that swimsuit?" Kim asked Jackie. We were all relaxing around the hotel pool before dinner. I noticed a few of the ladies from our tour group strolling around the pool. I knew they were with the National Parks Wonders Tour because, unlike us, they were wearing their nametags. They waved, and we waved back.

"I don't remember," Jackie said. "Why?"

"I like it and thought I might look for a similar one when we get home."

Jackie wrenched off her sunglasses. "You can't afford this suit, Kim. Anyway, I thought Eddie only allowed you to shop at Walmart."

Kim smiled, but I could see tension pull at her lips. "That's just a joke. I can buy whatever I want, wherever I want. I don't do hair as a hobby, you know. I earn a good living. And Eddie doesn't own me."

"Could have fooled me," Crystal blurted.

Kim's fists clenched at her sides. We were supposed to be relaxing, but she was wound tighter than a banjo string.

"Did you find your cell phone?" I asked to change the subject.

She held it up. "Yes, thank goodness. It was on the bathroom counter just as Jackie had thought."

I was about to ask the group what time they wanted to eat dinner when a familiar voice sounded behind us. "How's the water, ladies?"

We all turned our heads in tandem. There stood Keith, barefoot and in a pair of lightweight trunks and a tee shirt. A white towel was slung over one broad shoulder. His teeth practically sparkled in the sunlight when he smiled.

"The water's fine," Kim said, not knowing how the water was. She hadn't even dipped a toe in. "Going for a swim before dinner, Keith?" she asked, blinking like she did when she was nervous.

"Just a quick one," he answered, dropping the towel onto the lounger next to Crystal. When he winked at her, Crystal's face turned ten shades of pink. "I try to do some form of exercise every day, even when I'm on a tour. Gotta stay in shape, you know."

We all watched with our mouths hanging open as he stripped off the tee shirt and displayed a six-pack of rippled abs. No one seemed immune to his impressive physique, including me. Even the old ladies on the other side of the pool openly stared when he stepped onto the diving board and scored a flawless jackknife dive and an equally perfect splash. After swimming a half-dozen laps, he surfaced from the water and plowed his hands through his wet hair. When he pushed himself up and over the side of the pool, I thought every woman there was going to have a seizure.

Water rolled off his glistening body. "Boy, that water is refreshing!" he exclaimed. "You girls should join me."

"We're hardly girls anymore," Annette said, laying her paperback book in her lap and peering over her sunglasses.

"That's for sure," Crystal said. "Annette's

birthday is Sunday. She turns fifty."

Annette fired Crystal a look that would have made her head vaporize had Annette's eyeballs been laser beams.

"But she doesn't look it, does she?" Crystal added quickly.

Keith's eyebrows lifted, and his gaze locked on Annette. "No, I would have guessed a youthful forty at the most."

A shy expression washed over Annette's face and she smiled, obviously pleased.

Keith moved toward us, sprinkling us with water drops when he shook his head. "I like to celebrate when we have someone on tour with a birthday. We'll be in Jackson Hole, Wyoming on Sunday. How would you like to have a picnic in a beautiful park for your birthday, Annette?"

Her eyes lit up. "I wouldn't want you to go to any trouble."

"It's no trouble. If I'm really lucky, I might even be able to round up a cake. With your figure, you don't have to worry about the calories." When he winked, she actually blushed like a schoolgirl. He grabbed his towel from off the lounger where he'd tossed it and toweled his face. "Have a great evening, ladies, and get a good night's sleep. Tomorrow we hit the road! I look forward to seeing you all in the morning. We're going to have a great time together."

His gaze swept down the row of us and then he saluted. Like vultures eyeing prey, we all craned our heads around and gawked as he strutted away.

Like a bolt out of the blue, it suddenly occurred to me that I've always been mistrustful of extremely good-looking men. Guys like Keith Creswell get away with bad behavior because of their looks, and because there are silly women who can't believe a guy so delicious could really be extremely rotten.

CHAPTER FIVE
Annette

"Why didn't one of you stop me from ordering that fried ham and cheese sandwich *and* onion rings?" My intestines cramped on cue, and I groaned. "I should have known better. Grease has become my archenemy as I've gotten older."

Kim patted my hand. "Sorry, Teresa. We all have our crosses to bear as we age. Mine is lactose intolerance."

"I suffer from acid reflux," Donna chimed in.

Crystal added to the discussion. "My gout flares up if I eat food high in purines."

"Too bad you all don't have an iron stomach like mine." Jackie patted her flat tummy, and I stuck my tongue out at her. She could eat like a horse, and anything she wanted, and still never gain an ounce or suffer from a humiliating disorder such as irritable bowel syndrome. The aging process and natural effects of gravity hadn't affected her waistline or boobs any either. Her body was as trim and perky as a teenager, and the only one of us to order dessert. She finished off her hot fudge and whipped topping sundae and then let out a little burp. "Oops. Excuse me. That was good."

Sometimes I really hated Jackie.

We ate dinner at the Paradise Café, along with the majority of the other National Parks Wonders Tour travelers. I knew, because they all wore their nametags. There were forty of us total, not counting Keith and Wayne. As I glanced around, I noticed Chuck and Bill, AKA Romeo and Casanova, were sitting in a nearby booth enjoying the company of three white-haired ladies. Other groups sat together getting acquainted.

"What do we do now?" Donna asked when we finished our meals. "It's too early to hit the sack but too late to get tickets to a show."

"Everything's so expensive, anyway," Crystal said.

"We could take taxis to the strip and see the buildings lit up at night," Kim suggested.

Jackie stood up and slung her purse over her shoulder. "I'm going to gamble in the hotel casino. Who wants to join me?"

"Not me," Crystal said. "You know my therapist says I have an addictive personality. I could get sucked in and lose all my money."

"Come on," Jackie urged. "You're not going to lose all your money on slots. It'll be fun. I'll put the brakes on if I see you turning into a one-armed bandit junkie."

"I don't know…"

"I'll give you the money to start with."

Crystal jumped up. "In that case, what are we waiting for?"

"Are you guys coming?" Kim asked Annette and me as she and Donna rose from the table.

"I'll meet you there in a little while." My stomach

gripped like a lasso had been roped around my middle and was squeezed tight.

"I'll wait with Teresa," Annette said, probably noticing my face contort.

"Okay. Feel better." Kim and Donna blew kisses and left.

Annette pulled a bottle from her purse and handed me what looked suspiciously like a brown horse pill.

"What's this?" I asked.

"It's an enzyme capsule. All natural. Take it with water. It should help your problem."

"Thanks." I was willing to try anything, so I downed the pill with the remainder of my iced tea. Literally, within a matter of minutes, my cramps had dissipated. "You're either a miracle worker or a witch, Annette."

She chuckled. "More like a walking pharmacy." She opened her bag to show me three more pill bottles inside.

"What's all that?"

She lifted each bottle from her purse. "This one's for high cholesterol. This is for anxiety. And this one's to help me sleep at night."

I knew about her high cholesterol, which still surprised me because she was thin, but I hadn't realized the stress of her home life had driven her to the other pharmaceuticals. She shoved the bottles deep into her purse and changed the subject.

"Wasn't that nice of Keith to offer to buy a cake for my birthday on Sunday?"

"It certainly was. I have a feeling he does whatever it takes to make his travelers happy."

"Can you believe he thought I look ten years

younger than I am?" Annette chuckled and rolled her eyes, but I could see Keith's comment had made an impact.

I wondered how long it had been since a man had paid her a compliment. From what she'd shared with me, Bruce left early each morning and worked late every night. When he was home, he rarely paid attention to her. They hadn't had sex in months. To add to her woes, Dustin, their twenty-six-year-old son, was unemployed and on the brink of divorce and had moved back into the house. From the tears I'd seen her cry lately, he was too angry and self-absorbed to speak politely to his mother, let alone say something nice.

Although she was educated and held a professional job as a paralegal, I'd watched Annette's confidence slip in the past year. Now that I knew she might be dependent upon pills to help her cope, I was worried.

"Has Dustin got any job prospects?" I asked, feeling things might be better if her loser of a son wasn't in the house adding to her stress.

She shook her head. "No, but I don't want to talk about Dustin on this trip, if that's okay with you. Or Bruce, either."

I nodded. "No problem. But you know I'm always here if you ever need to get things off your chest."

She smiled. "Thanks, Teresa. You've always been a good friend, not only to me, but to all of us. You're the only one who has her act together. We're all turning fifty this year, and each one of us is struggling with some issue, except you. How do you do it?"

"Do what?"

"Manage to be happy and content with your life."

I shrugged. "I've always accepted the hand I've been dealt. Less drama that way."

"Even in high school I admired you," Annette continued. "You never worried about what other people thought of you. I wanted to be more like that, but I'd been instilled with a different set of values. My whole world revolved around being pretty, popular, and making sure I had a date every Saturday night."

What I remembered was how Annette's mother had pushed her into beauty contests and local modeling gigs as a little girl. By the time she was in high school, it was clear that Annette felt any love and praise she received at home depended on her making the cheerleading squad, Homecoming court, and being voted the Most Popular or Best Looking in the class.

"Remember when Bruce and I broke up right before the prom of our senior year?" she ruminated. "I thought my world had ended. Mom was so disappointed that I couldn't hang onto my popular boyfriend."

That had been a terrible time for Annette. Bruce had dumped her, briefly, for the football coach's daughter. "You and I were each other's date," I recalled, chuckling and trying to make light of a situation that had occurred decades ago. "We even had our picture taken together under the archway of flowers."

She laughed. "I was so afraid everyone thought we'd become gay. How stupid was I, anyway?"

"You weren't stupid. Too concerned about perfection maybe, but your mom drilled that into you. Annette, you were always an intelligent person and still are." Except for marrying Bruce the month after high school graduation, I thought. Even at eighteen and standing as a bridesmaid in their wedding, I foresaw the train wreck their marriage was to become.

"As a young mother, you went to school and became a paralegal," I continued. "Not many women have the determination, brains, guts, and energy to take on such a big challenge. You career is still going strong, and you didn't achieve that success because of the way you look." Shapely with long dark hair, blue eyes, and flawless skin, Annette was still a beautiful woman.

"Thanks, Teresa. You should have been a cheerleader in high school. You know exactly what to say to pep people up when they're down."

"It's a gift," I said, smiling.

Our conversation halted while we said hello to some of our fellow travelers as they strolled past our table.

"Aren't you with our tour?" one of the elderly ladies asked. From her nametag, I saw her name was Winnie.

"Yes, we are."

"A group of us are going to soak in the hot tub out by the pool and enjoy some frozen cocktails. Would you care to join us?"

I looked at Annette. "I'm feeling better. What do you think?"

"Take a walk on the wild side," another lady named Doris said. "We're old, but you'll find we're a lot of fun."

A grin filled Annette's face. "Thanks for the invitation. Sounds like a great way to start this vacation. We'll go upstairs and change into our swimsuits and be right out."

The ladies said they'd order us each a strawberry daiquiri from the pool bar.

Before Annette and I slipped into our separate rooms to change, her eyes sparkled, and she said, "I feel like this is the first day of the rest of my life."

I gave her a hug and hoped she wouldn't need one of those sleeping pills that night.

CHAPTER SIX
Crystal

I'd never been in a hot tub before, but the tingly feeling that ran through my arms and legs almost reminded me of a pot high. It had been years since I'd smoked, but you never forget those magical sensations. I quite liked how soaking in bubbling hot water for an hour reduced my mind to a mushy mass of warm oatmeal.

"Are you guys drunk?" Crystal's loud voice jarred me out of my happy, semi-lucid state. A pair of flip-flops smacked across the concrete to stop dangerously close to my head. The moment I twisted my neck and looked up, the jets located behind my back surged and sent a pleasant jolt through my body. When I squealed, Annette and the five ladies we shared the hot tub with roared with laughter.

Crystal nudged my shoulder blade with her foot and repeated, "Are you drunk?"

"We're all drunk, honey!" Doris exclaimed. Again, we laughed.

"Looks like you're having a better time than we did," Jackie droned.

I craned my head around to the other side and saw

Jackie, Donna and Kim standing next to Crystal. They looked like four little ducks in a row. "You didn't hit the jackpot?" I asked.

"No," Donna answered. "It's a good thing we're leaving Vegas tomorrow. We practically had to pull Crystal off the slot machine kicking and screaming."

"I told you I can get addicted quickly," she replied sourly. "Nothing good ever happens to me. I thought my luck might change if I kept playing. I was so close to winning!"

"The only thing you were close to was getting thrown out of the joint for carrying on like a lunatic." Jackie turned on her heel. "I'm going to bed. Are you coming, roomie?"

Kim nodded. "Keith said he'd see us bright-eyed and bushy-tailed in the morning. That means getting our beauty rest."

"We don't want to disappoint him," Donna added with a smile.

Annette's swimsuit made a swooshing sound when she rose from the hot tub and reached for her towel. "I'll go with you guys. Getting up early to travel, and being in the hot sun all day has caught up with me. Soaking in the Jacuzzi has made me even more sleepy."

"Party poopers," one of the older ladies teased.

"Are you coming?" Donna asked me, as she wrapped the towel around her shivering shoulders.

"I have my key. I'll be there soon. My bones want to enjoy just a few more minutes of heaven."

"You guys go on. I'll stay here with Teresa," Crystal said, waving goodbye to our friends. Once they'd left, she slipped off her flip-flops and sat on the edge of the hot tub. When she dangled her feet into the steamy water, she let out a small moan. "Wow, that feels wonderful. I should have joined you all instead of letting Jackie talk me into gambling."

I introduced her to Winnie, Doris, Joyce, Barb, and Norma, more retired teachers, all from Florida.

"What do you do?" Joyce asked Crystal. "We already got the low-down on Teresa and Annette."

"I drive a school bus."

"You don't say?" The ladies nodded to each other, impressed. "We know how awful kids can be since we were teachers. How do you keep those monkeys in line?"

"I threaten to sit on them if they don't behave."

The ladies, all roughly the same size as Crystal, laughed. Even though she joked about her weight, it was all a façade. Crystal had married later in life, having met her ex-husband at a church singles club. Then Greg lost religion and left her six years ago for another woman. His excuse was Crystal had gotten fat. His cruelty had hurt her deeply, and her self-esteem still hadn't recovered.

"Are you married?" Barb asked.

That was a subject Crystal tried her best to avoid at all costs. On cue, her hand fluttered to her chest. "Hot flash!" she cried.

Once again, the ladies all nodded. "We've been there," Barb said. She scooped ice cubes from her Tom Collins drink and offered them to Crystal. "Rub these over your face and chest. They'll cool you down."

"Best decision I ever made was to get a hysterectomy," Norma said, "but I had no idea I'd go into early menopause immediately after the surgery."

"Night sweats were the worst," Winnie declared.

"My sex life went down the tubes when I started menopause," Doris added.

Joyce smacked her arm playfully. "Mine improved! When my husband learned he no longer had to worry about getting me pregnant, he couldn't get enough."

Barb chimed in again. "I remember my doctor telling me I should try to have sex more often because it increases blood flow to the hoo-ha and helps keep the tissues healthy."

My narrowed gaze connected with Crystal's. All this menopause talk sobered me up in a New York minute.

"I didn't mean to start these ladies talking about their sex lives," Crystal whispered behind her hand. "I just wanted to distract them from the subject of my failed marriage."

"Well, you certainly did that."

"Would it be rude for us to leave?"

I shook my head and made our apologies. "Will you excuse us, ladies? We're going back to our rooms. It's been a long day, and the rooster will crow early in the morning." Crystal gave me a hand out of the hot tub and I wrapped my gigantic beach towel around my body. "You really are a bunch of fun broads. See you tomorrow at breakfast or on the bus."

"Good night," they called to our backs.

Once we stepped inside the hotel and were well out of earshot, Crystal and I broke down and laughed until tears ran down our faces. "Those women are firecrackers," she said.

"I expect we'll be just like them when we're that

age. Once you reach a certain point in your life, there's no reason not to be honest and say whatever you want. Of course, I usually say what's on my mind, anyway."

"You've never minced words, even when we were kids," Crystal said.

I hurried Crystal past the 24-hour casino as we made our way to the elevator. "What can I say? I was born an opinionated big mouth."

She smiled. "I wish I was as secure as you. The five of us could all take lessons from you about having confidence."

I pushed the elevator button and frowned. "I wish y'all would knock me off the pedestal you've placed me on. I'm not perfect, you know. I have faults, a lot of them. Why do you think I've never been married?"

The elevator door opened and we stepped inside. "You could have married," she replied. "Dale was crazy about you. So was Curt. Both of them were good guys. I never understood why you broke off your engagements. Have you missed not being a wife and mother? I miss being a wife, and I wanted children desperately. Now it's too late."

Not intending to engage in the same conversation I'd had with Crystal countless times since her divorce, I stared at the light above the door and tapped my foot as the elevator slowly made its way to the tenth floor.

"Is Phil a good kisser?" she blurted as the door opened on our floor.

We stepped into the deserted hallway and I whispered, "I didn't think you knew about him. We've been careful to keep our trysts covert."

She whispered back. "You can't keep that kind of secret from one of your best friends, Teresa. Sure I know about Phil, but I respect you enough not to ask questions since it's obvious you don't want to confide in me." She put on her hurt face.

"I share plenty with you. But my relationships are personal and private, especially with Phil. That's how he and I prefer it."

I walked Crystal to her door, which was two doors down from mine. The air conditioning in the hotel was freezing. My body quivered as I stood in the hallway in my wet swimsuit and damp towel. "Why did you ask about kissing?"

"Sex was never that great with Greg," she answered. "It started going downhill a few years after our wedding, but Greg never wanted to talk about our problems. I figured I wasn't sexy enough for him since I gained a few pounds. At least he always made me feel like *I* was the problem, not him. In the months leading up to his leaving, we didn't go to bed without him making a snide comment about my *thunder thighs* or *jelly belly*. The truth was, he was a selfish jerk, in bed and out. I don't miss him, but I do miss kissing a man. You should thank your lucky stars you get kissed regularly."

I thought about the way Phil's mustache tickles when he kisses me. He was a great kisser. In fact, on a scale from one to ten, he was a solid twelve. Crystal was right. I'd miss kissing, too, if I couldn't count on it frequently.

"When I was a kid," she continued, "I practiced kissing using my pillow. Did you ever do that?"

"Sure. Didn't everyone practice that way?"

"I don't know. We didn't talk about stuff like that when we were kids. Anyway, I haven't kissed a man in over three years. And I'm as parched as this Nevada desert for that kind of intimacy."

"Three years?" I tried to remember whom she'd dated last. Had it been that long ago? "You went out with that guy from Champaign for awhile. Didn't you ever kiss him?"

She blew me a raspberry. "He didn't even try until the fourth date. Then when he finally screwed up the courage, he mashed his lips on mine and they felt like wet Jello with a side of slobber. To add insult to injury, his tongue awkwardly probed my mouth like a darting snake. Nauseated, I had to push him away. Honestly, I almost puked on his shoes. Needless to say, I never saw him again. Kissing is that important to me."

"Oh, Crystal, I'm sorry. You're going to meet the right guy someday. It'll happen when you least expect it." I squeezed her arm hoping my small act of empathy would be enough for the night. I'd given her this same pep talk before. Right then, my teeth chattered and my leg jumped because I needed to pee. If I caught pneumonia, I was going to send her the hospital bill.

She stared at my dancing leg. "I can tell you're cold. I'll let you go change and get to bed. Sorry for boring you with my sad tales."

No one was better at gentle manipulation than Crystal. Fortunately, I knew her game well and wouldn't be intimidated by guilt. "Good night and sweet dreams," I said cheerfully while shuffling toward my door.

"Maybe I'll dream about Keith," she whispered. "Now there's a man I'd like to do some serious lip locking with."

A vision flashed through my mind of the two of them. I didn't know why at the time, but the image of Crystal and our tour director together gave me a creepy feeling; like someone had walked over my grave. Of course, as you already know, turns out it wasn't *my* grave we'd be talking about at the end of our vacation.

CHAPTER SEVEN
Heavenly Bodies

Air conditioning, reclining seats, televisions, and an on board restroom made traveling aboard the motor coach more comfortable than I'd expected. Energy and excitement sizzled through the bus on our first day out as Wayne sped alongside Utah's Virgin River.

Keith stood at the front of the bus wearing khaki shorts and a muscle-hugging tee shirt talking into a portable microphone. "We'll be driving about twenty-five hundred miles on this tour. Our first stop will be in St. George, where we'll pick up food for a picnic lunch later. Then we'll head to Utah's first national park, the beautiful Zion National, which means heavenly place of God. While there, we'll be following the paths where ancient native people and pioneers walked and where massive sandstone cliffs of cream, pink, and red soar into a brilliant blue sky. When we stop tonight, we'll be at an altitude of almost eight thousand feet."

He then regaled us with scary stories about how altitude sickness has affected people on his past tours. Twice I've lost my lunch while on boats and hoped the high altitudes wouldn't affect me in the same way.

"Tonight we'll be staying near Bryce Canyon at a

place called Ruby's Inn," he continued. "For those who are interested, you can watch bronco busters and cowboys display their skills as they perform in a rodeo starting at seven o'clock."

"Will the cowboys be as handsome as you?" a woman called out. I craned my head to see it was Doris who spoke. Chuckles sifted through the bus, and Keith flashed a disarming grin.

"Are you flirting with me, Doris, you little cougar?"

She clawed the air with her fingers and roared her response, causing us all to laugh again.

It was impressive that we were on our first day out and Keith seemed to have put names to faces already. Although his gaze brushed over everyone as people began raising their hands and asking questions about the itinerary, I noticed his eyes kept focusing on Jackie. I was sitting next to her, and we were two rows behind where he stood. My observation of him was as subtle as his attempt to catch her attention. When I saw their gazes connect and she smiled her cat smile, I elbowed her in the rib—hard.

"Wouldn't your husband just love to see a rodeo, Jackie?" Shameless, I said it loud enough for Keith to hear. "You'd probably have to tie him down to keep him from trying to ride one of those bulls." I swallowed a chuckle at imagining poor old Milton astride a bucking horse or bull. Jackie's fiery eyes stabbed at me like daggers, but I didn't care. I think I made my point. Keith's gaze flicked away.

When we arrived at the park, the bus door swung open. "We're here!" Wayne announced. "Everyone watch your step as you exit the coach."

Keith jaunted to the bottom of the steps. "Feel free to wander the area on your own," he said to each person as we trailed off the bus. "We'll meet in front of the Zion lodge for a picnic lunch at noon." He offered his assistance as I wobbled on the steps (my foot had gone to sleep and hadn't woken up yet) and then he reached for Jackie's hand. I noticed he held her hand a little longer than was necessary. "Be sure to check out the emerald pools and waterfall," he told her. "The pools are almost as clear and green as your eyes."

"We'll be sure to. Thanks for the tip," she replied, flipping on her sunglasses and swinging her hips like a pendulum as she walked away. My body was still in pretty good shape, but if I moved my hips that way, I'd be flat on my back for a day.

"Let's check out the visitors center over there," Donna said, grabbing my arm and pulling me that way. Our friends followed. Inside, we watched a short video and then stood on a deck outside the building to gaze upon the red sandstone peaks, one of which was called the Watchman. Behind the Watchmen was the West Temple. According to the brochure, it rose 3800 feet. Along the Watchman Trail, we got an excellent view of the Towers of the Virgin, which included the Sundial, the Meridian Tower, and the Alter of Sacrifice.

"Have you ever seen anything so stunning?" Annette asked, clearly in awe—as we all were.

Kim skimmed through a pamphlet about the park. "According to this, some people claim to see the shrouded figure of the Virgin Mary on the face of the peak."

The rugged beauty of the peaks and cliffs had us

mesmerized. Surprisingly, no one even cracked a single joke about virgins.

After hiking up to the emerald pools and waterfall and back, it was time for lunch. The grounds in front of the Zion lodge were full of tourists picnicking. Wayne and Keith were stationed at a picnic table handing out sack lunches to our group that the two of them had put together.

"Did you see the waterfall?" Keith asked Jackie when we approached.

"Yes, but my feet are killing me after all the walking." She pointed to her impractical sandals. "I'll have to wear different shoes from now on."

"There's a lot of walking on this tour," he said. "Tennis shoes are recommended, unless you brought along a personal masseuse to rub your feet at night."

Always the flirt, Jackie took advantage of his comment. She batted her eyelashes and cooed, "Perhaps you could recommend someone with strong hands."

When I shoved her out of the way and reached for my sack lunch, Keith shrugged and smiled. "Hope you like what we packed for you."

"What you're packing looks just fine to me," Jackie said under her breath. There was no way Keith could have missed the way she looked him up and down before I wheeled her away.

"Get a grip," I groaned. "You're not a cat in heat." I dragged her toward a group from our tour that was sitting on the grass. The five ladies Donna and I had shared a hot tub with were there, as were Romeo and Casanova.

"Hey, girls!" Chuck called. "Sit with us and rest

your bones." He waved his sandwich in the air.

"Hi, everyone." I sat cross-legged in the grass hoping I'd be able to get up again when it came time. Jackie spread her napkin onto the grass before sitting so she wouldn't get her white shorts dirty. We dug into our lunches of sandwiches and chips. After all the hiking we'd done, I was famished and thirsty.

"Have you seen our friends?" I asked the group after downing half of my bottled water in one long swallow.

Someone pointed to another circle of people not far away. "They're over there getting to know more of the people in our group."

Donna and Annette seemed to be enjoying a conversation with a couple we'd learned was from Australia. Crystal was mugging for someone with a camera, and Kim was holding her cell phone into the air, probably trying to get some bars.

Jackie saw her, too, and rolled her eyes. "Look at Kim trying to find a cell phone connection out here. Honestly, she's worse than a teenager the way she constantly has that phone glued to her ear. I don't know why she feels the need to check in with Eddie so often. I've never understood what she sees in him."

I shot Jackie a look that suggested she shouldn't be airing our friend's business in front of strangers.

"She must be in love and likes to hear his voice," Barb said. "I remember that feeling, although it's been a while."

"Or maybe she's calling to check up on him," Winnie added with a knowing look. "Although he never cheated, as far as I know, my deceased husband had a wandering eye. Your friend might be worried about what her man is doing when she's not around."

I knew that to be closer to the truth, but I wasn't about to talk behind Kim's back.

"He hasn't got a penny to his name," Jackie said, nibbling a cookie. "And believe me, he's no looker. No one would want him."

"There's more to love than money and looks," Chuck said, peering from under the rim of his golf cap.

Jackie laughed. "Not in my world, Chuck."

"Are you married?" Norma asked her.

Jackie flashed her ten-carat diamond in response.

"Darn," Chuck grumbled. "Why are all the cute ones hitched?"

"I'm single and cute," Doris piped up, winking at Chuck. Despite her feisty attitude and good personality, she was short and shaped like a bowling ball. He ignored her and bit into his sandwich.

"Your husband must be very wealthy to afford a ring that size," Norma said, peering closer. "Is he terribly handsome, too? I expect he resembles a movie star, since you're so young and beautiful."

Jackie batted her eyelashes like the southern belle she wasn't. "Thank you for the compliment, Norma! You all may not believe this, but I'm turning fifty in a few months. My friends and I are on this trip as a way to celebrate our upcoming milestones. Annette's the first of us. Her birthday is on Sunday."

I noticed how she easily deflected Norma's question about her husband.

"Fifty!" Joyce slapped her thigh. "That seems like a lifetime ago for me. What a terrific way for you ladies to commemorate surviving half a century of living."

"Gee, that makes us sound ancient," I chuckled.

Joyce asked Winnie for a hand up. I heard her bones creak. "Wait until you're on the other side of seventy and then talk to me about ancient," she said, grabbing at her back.

"Joyce, you don't look a day over sixty-nine," Chuck joked. We all laughed, and I noticed the sweet smile she graced him with.

"Do you all like to dance?" Jackie asked, changing the subject altogether. Their gray and white heads bobbed up and down. She stood up and put her fingers between her lips and whistled. When Kim, Crystal, Donna and Annette glanced our way, she waved them over. "My girlfriends and I will show you folks what we do in Illinois for fun every Monday night."

After coaxing Crystal to let down her inhibitions and be spontaneous, the six of us proceeded to sing a cappella (mostly off-key) while we line danced to Tim McGraw's *I Like It I Love It* in front of our new friends and any other tourists wanting a good chuckle.

When our performance ended, we received a standing ovation and thunderous applause. We smiled and bowed in appreciation. That day was our first line dancing show on the National Parks Wonders Tour, but it wouldn't be the last.

"That's what I call shaking your booty," Chuck said, clapping the hardest.

I already liked our fellow travelers and guessed I'd have at least a dozen new laugh lines on my face by the end of the trip. What I didn't expect would be the accompanying worry lines. But killing someone does that to you.

CHAPTER EIGHT
Whoa, Cowgirl!

There are some women who can look at a man and realize he's no damn good and still think all he needs is the right woman to love him. She thinks she can love that loser better than anyone else can and nobody can tell her any different. For a young woman, that lesson can be a tough one to learn, but for women our age, it's just plain ridiculous.

When we were in high school, Crystal had a poster on her wall that said: *YOU HAVE TO KISS A LOT OF TOADS BEFORE YOU FIND YOUR PRINCE.* I was sitting in a booth in Ruby's Cowboy Steak and Buffet Room with Annette, Barb and Joyce eating my dinner of ribs and a couple of sides of carbs. As I observed the hustle and bustle around me, I thought about that proverb.

In another booth across the room, Jackie and Keith sat side-by-side chatting and laughing. Bill and another lady I hadn't met yet were their booth mates, but they seemed to be lost in their own conversation. I swallowed a bite of macaroni salad and stared at Jackie.

She'd certainly kissed her share of toads through

the years. Although Milton had been a nice man before his mind went, and he'd given her every material thing she'd ever dreamed of, he was a far cry from the prince of her girlhood dreams.

I pierced a chunk of meat with my fork and wondered if Chris Stevens was a prince or a pig dog. Was he missing Jackie while she was on this trip? Had she called him since we'd left Illinois? She hadn't mentioned him, and I honestly didn't know if their relationship was serious or just another fling. My gut told me Chris was another toad in a long string of Jackie's amphibians.

When she caught me watching her, she waved. Keith looked over and waved, too. I smiled and hoped their friendly flirting wouldn't escalate into more.

"Hey, Teresa, you're going to the rodeo, aren't you?" Annette asked, drawing me out of my reverie. She wiped her mouth with a napkin and pushed back from the table with her hand on her stomach.

"Heck, yeah I'm going. I've never been to a rodeo before. I want to experience everything the Wild West has to offer."

"I think we should change out of shorts and into jeans though," she said. "Wayne told me it can get cool in Utah at night."

"All right." Just then, Donna and Crystal stepped up to our table and we informed them of our plans. "Where's Kim?" I asked.

Donna answered. "She's browsing in the gift shop and said she'll meet us out front in twenty minutes."

We stopped at Jackie's booth on our way out of the restaurant. She told us she'd catch up with us at the rodeo.

"We'll see you there, too," Bill said. "By the way, this is Violet."

We said hello to Violet. When we introduced ourselves, we learned she was a widow from New York.

"I came on this tour with my sister, Daisy," Violet said. "She's around here somewhere."

"Have a good time at the rodeo," Keith said. "Everyone always does."

We left the foursome, and when I looked over my shoulder before turning the corner, I saw Jackie squeeze Keith's arm. Gooseflesh peppered my arm, and I shook my head.

As we passed by the gift shop, I decided to purchase some post cards for my scrapbook. "I'll be up to change into jeans and grab my sweater in a few minutes," I told my roomie, Donna.

Strolling straight to the rack of postcards, I thought of Phil while thumbing through them. I hadn't called him since leaving Harley's Grove and had no plans to. Our relationship wasn't like that. We didn't check in with each other or talk on the phone like silly teenagers. Ours was a mature relationship based mostly on sex. It was true he liked to cook for me, and as I've mentioned already, we went shooting together. But we mostly enjoyed the physical pleasures we offered each other without strings attached. It was an arrangement we were both comfortable with, except that I'd been wondering about Phil lately.

Feeling sentimental when recalling the moony look that had shone in his eyes when he kissed me goodbye the night before I left for Vegas, I decided he might appreciate getting a postcard from me in the mail. I chose two of the same card (one for him and one for my scrapbook). It had cowboys and stampeding horses on the front with the caption reading *The Great American West*.

On my way to the cash register, I almost changed my mind about purchasing a memento for him. The image of Harley Grove's nosy mail carrier, Gwen, flashed in my mind. As soon as she saw a postcard from me to Phil, tongues would wag. Gwen was the biggest busy body in town. Handling everyone's mail just made her side job as village gossip easier.

"Oh, hell," I mumbled to myself. "Let them talk." I slapped the postcards on the counter and reached into my wallet to pay.

Before heading to the door, I searched the aisles for Kim. I'd almost given up thinking she'd already left when I spied her. In a far corner of the store, she stood alone with her back to me. Her head jerked from side to side as if she were on the lookout for someone. Slipping quietly up behind her, I tickled her ribs and said, "Boo."

The items in her hand dropped to the floor, and she let out a soft strangled scream. Her eyes enlarged when she spun around and our gazes met. "Why are you sneaking up on me like that, Teresa?" she barked. "I almost peed my shorts."

"Sorry. We're getting ready to go to the rodeo. You want to go?"

She inhaled a deep breath. "Sure." Grabbing my arm, she tried to spin me away, but I escaped her grip.

"You dropped your stuff." I bent and picked up three small Kodak boxes. "What do you need film for? Isn't your camera digital?"

"Those aren't mine," she said, snatching the boxes from my hand and tossing them into the bin in front of her. "Come on, let's get out of here."

"Whatever." As she pulled me out of the gift shop, a shiver ran down my spine. She'd dropped those boxes of film when I scared her. I'd seen her drop them. Why did she lie? What was Kim hiding?

~ * ~

Turned out, the rodeo participants were mostly local kids and teenagers, which was disappointing for Doris and her cronies. They'd been hoping to get a quick thrill salivating over mature cowboy man meat. The five amigas, as we started calling the retired ladies from Florida, sat on the bleacher behind me, all wearing matching straw cowboy hats and looking as cute as dolls.

"Why didn't we buy cowboy hats?" I asked my friends.

"We're not cowgirls," Crystal answered.

"There are plenty of cows around Harley's Grove," I said. "And everyone we've met says we look young enough to be girls. That should qualify us to be cowgirls."

Crystal screamed and bolted up from her seat when a young rider got bucked off a snot-nosed bull and was nearly horned in the buttocks before scrambling up the rails of the fence to safety. When the excitement was over, she lowered her weight onto the bench again. "That was a close one. These kids have more guts in their pinkie fingers than I do in my entire body."

"Hey, Teresa, do you remember those guys from Iowa that we hung out with the summer after we graduated high school?" Donna asked. "They were on the construction crew building the new seed plant outside of town."

"How could I forget them?" I said, leaning across Annette to talk to Donna. "That jerk, Scott, stole my guitar and left town and never returned."

"Didn't you date him for a while? He was kind of cute in a long-haired lanky kind of way."

"Cute, but weird. And yes, we went on a couple of dates. Once he took me to the Smorgasbord in Bloomington for dinner. I was so embarrassed I didn't tell anyone. My folks used to go there for lunch after church on Sundays!"

I thought back to those days. There had been six guys Donna and I met cruising Main Street, and between us we'd dated all of them at some point that summer. Scott had been strange, so of course, he gravitated toward me. All the weird ones did back then.

I remembered swimming with him and a couple of the other guys in the community pool one afternoon. Scott kept plunging under the water near me. It wasn't until one of the other guys pulled me aside and said Scott was beaver hunting that I realized his reason for going underwater. He was trying to look up my swimsuit. *Pig.*

"What made you think of them?" I asked Donna.

"Randy wore a cowboy hat and boots all the time."

"Oh, yeah, I remember. He was nice in a chunky fresh-faced kind of way." I smiled, recalling more crazy times we had with those Iowa guys. I pressed my hand on Annette's thigh and leaned farther over her. "Donna, do you remember the night Randy drove us through somebody's cornfield in his big four-wheel pickup?"

Her mouth broadened into a grin. "Yes. The three of us were crammed into the cab of his truck, along with his friend with the red hair. I think they were both drunk. Randy must have ruined that farmer's whole crop. Cornstalks were flying everywhere and bouncing off the windshield."

We both laughed.

"It's a wonder you didn't get arrested," Annette said.

"Yes, it's a miracle a lot of things didn't happen that summer." Donna and I stopped chuckling and locked gazes. One of those things I was referring to was her own close call. She'd missed a period after sleeping with Randy and had thought she was pregnant. Fortunately, it was a false alarm.

"Way to go!" Crystal hooted, halting our reminiscing. A teenage girl apparently ran the barrel race in record time. As the girl accepted her award, the crowd around us applauded.

I glanced at Kim, who blankly stared at the activity going on in the ring and seemed lost in her own world. My mind drifted back to what had happened in the gift shop and then further back to New Year's Eve when that box from her closet had nearly knocked my block off. Worry niggled at me, but whatever it was that bothered her—and me—this wasn't the time or place to talk about it.

"Kim, where's Jackie?" I asked instead. "I

thought she was meeting us here at the rodeo."

Kim snapped out of her daydream. "She was laying on the bed when I left our room. Said she had a bad headache and may not make it."

"Oh. That's too bad. She's missing out on a lot of fun." My gaze returned to the rodeo ring. I robotically clapped when one clown dumped a bucket of paper graffiti over the head of another clown, but my mind traveled elsewhere. I was hoping Jackie wasn't doing something idiotic.

Of course, if I'd known then what I learned later about what she'd been up to that night, I'd have moved hell and earth to stop her. Because, what she did was just the start of a series of events that led to Keith's unfortunate demise.

CHAPTER NINE
HooDoo You Trust?

The next morning, our first stop was Bryce Canyon National Park, distinctive for its unique geology. As we exited the motor coach, Keith gathered the group around. He wore a pair of dark sunglasses, which wasn't surprising since it was sunny out. The fact that he hadn't removed them while inside the bus earlier seemed odd since the windows were tinted. But the thought was fleeting at the time.

"Bryce Canyon consists of a series of horseshoe-shaped amphitheaters carved from the eastern edge of the Paunsaugunt Plateau," he explained. "The erosional force of frost-wedging and the dissolving power of rainwater have shaped the colorful limestone rock into bizarre shapes, including slot canyons, windows, and these beautiful red and orange spires behind me called hoodoos."

When I gazed at the scenery that seemed to stretch for miles beyond, the breath literally left my throat. I'd never seen anything like those rock hoodoos.

Keith went on. "The Paiute legend is that these spiral pillars are men who were turned to stone by an angry deity and are condemned to stand forever in silence."

When his recitation was over, everyone headed off in different directions to explore. Crystal tugged on my hand pulling me to the Bryce Point sign showing we were at an elevation of 8300 feet. A group of Harley bikers were taking their pictures in front of it.

"I want you to take my photo here," she said, sizing up the male bikers that were clad in black clothes and boots, despite the heat that had already climbed into the eighties.

My eyebrow cocked. "You just want to meet those men."

"Sure I do. Don't you? They look interesting."

Although I've never been into bikers, a memory flashed in my mind of riding on the back of some guy's motorcycle when I was eighteen or nineteen. We'd made out by the pond on the edge of town under the moonlight of a summer Saturday night. I have no idea what his name was. Never saw him again.

"Want us to take your picture in front of this sign?" one of the bikers asked, walking toward us. He was a bear of a man with a straggly red beard, a black leather cap on his head, and chains hanging from around his ample waist. Sweat glistened his ruddy face.

"Thanks!" Crystal chirped, handing him her camera. I handed mine to his buddy and they snapped our picture together.

"Where are you ladies from?" the bear asked, returning the camera.

Crystal offered him a bright smile. "Illinois. We're here with a tour group. We started in Vegas, are visiting several national parks, and ending up in Mount Rushmore. What about you?"

He nodded to his friends who looked equally hot (as in sweating like hogs, not attractive). "The ten of us are traveling two thousand miles through Arizona and Utah sightseeing."

"Sounds interesting. Where have you been so far?"

Before he could answer, I yanked on her arm. "Have a good time," I told Bear.

She hollered "goodbye" over her shoulder and then frowned at my rudeness. "What'd you do that for?"

"Because Mr. Bad Ass Bear isn't your Prince Charming. There's no sense in wasting time chatting him up." I suspected Crystal was hoping to accidentally bump into her soul mate on this trip. Or maybe she was more desperate than I thought for any kind of attention. But bikers who didn't have the sense to wear something other than black leather in June in Utah didn't deserve more than a passing glance, in my opinion.

She walked away with a "Hmmph."

After we'd taken pictures of Sunset Point and Thor's Hammer and more hoodoos than you could imagine, we were back on the bus tooling down the highway toward Salt Lake City. Keith stood up and announced it was time to officially introduce ourselves. Then we'd watch a video about the Grand Tetons, which we'd be seeing in a couple of days. My friends and I had occupied the first two rows of seats behind Keith since the start of the trip, and there we sat again, so it was natural for him to begin the introduction game with us.

He pointed to Jackie. "Let's start with you. Please stand up here in front so everyone can see you and tell us your name, where you're from, your occupation, your hobbies, your favorite places you've traveled to, and your brush with fame."

Jackie's hesitation and icy stare sent a clear signal that she and Keith were no longer as friendly as they'd been last night. "Come on," he urged, reaching out to touch her arm. She jerked it away.

When she finally slipped out of the seat, she stood as far away from him as she could and refused to take the microphone from his hand. "My name is Jackie," she began, speaking loudly so the people in the back could hear. "I'm from Illinois, and I don't have an occupation because I'm married to a rich man." That got a few chuckles. "My hobby is shopping (more chuckles), my favorite place I've traveled to is Italy, and my brush with fame was shaking hands with Anson Williams of the TV show, Happy Days, when I was fifteen years old. He was performing at King's Island near Cincinnati at the time. That's it. Thank you."

She moved past Keith without looking at him and crawled over the top of her seat mate, Donna. Then she stared out the window with her arms crossed over her chest. Jackie never was able to hide her feelings. I didn't know what had happened between her and Keith, but her little scene didn't seem to faze him one bit. Ever the professional, he pleasantly said, "You're next" to Donna.

"Hi, everyone," she spoke into his microphone. "I'm Donna, and I'm also from Illinois. My occupation is office secretary at our local high school, the same school I attended. This is the first trip I've taken since going to Wisconsin on my honeymoon almost thirty years ago, so all the places we're seeing on this vacation are my favorite places to travel to, I guess. You see, I was widowed a year and a half ago, and my husband never liked to travel. I shouldn't have spent the money on this trip because I don't have any extra to squander, but I couldn't let down my friends. And I really wanted to visit the west. Now I'm going to need to win the lottery or discover gold in Yellowstone in order to pay my bills when I get home."

Uh-oh. Donna was rambling and sharing way more than this game required. "What was your brush with fame?" I hollered, attempting to steer her back on track.

She blushed and said, "I have an autographed photo of Jim Nabors from when he played Gomer Pyle on television. Does that count?"

Again, more laughs.

By the time everyone on the bus had played the introduction game, I was sleepy and barely stayed awake to watch the first half of the video on the Tetons. After a stop for lunch and another word and number game, we finally reached Salt Lake City.

We were given a tour of Mormon Temple Square and the lovely grounds that bloomed with pristine landscaping and bright flowers. Then we saw the Assembly Hall and the Tabernacle, where the world-famous choir performed, only not that day. Our two missionary guides were young women from Brazil and Germany.

"Those girls sure are passionate about their faith,"

Annette whispered to me as we walked around the visitor center sipping lemonade. "I wish I had something to be that passionate about."

I nodded, not really paying attention. My gaze was latched onto Donna, who was across the room talking to Keith. She listened intently to whatever he was saying. I wondered how long their conversation had lasted, because I sensed they were at the end of it. All of a sudden, she smiled and her head bobbed enthusiastically, and they shook hands. Before she stepped away, Keith placed his palm on Donna's shoulder. He said something else and she nodded again. Whatever he'd said, it seemed to make Donna very happy. Darn! I wished I could read lips.

"What is it about a good looking man that will turn a woman into jelly?" I grumbled aloud.

"Huh?" Annette stared at me quizzically.

I tossed my hand into the air. "Oh, never mind."

~ * ~

On the way to the Sheraton where we were to spend the night, Wayne drove us past the Beehive House and Lion House. Those homes had been where all of Brigham Young's wives lived back in the day.

"I can't manage to snag one wife," Keith joked. "Doesn't seem fair Brigham Young had so many." His joke caused several women to sigh, but I wasn't one of them. My suspicions were beginning to mount.

Life on the road probably made maintaining a relationship difficult for someone like Keith, but I doubted he lacked for female companionship. My curiosity piqued, and I wondered what had happened between him and Jackie to make her completely ignore him today. I was also interested in what he'd been talking to Donna about earlier.

After settling into our rooms and eating a mediocre dinner in the hotel restaurant, some of our new friends decided to head downtown for the evening, including Jackie, Crystal, Annette and Kim.

"I'm tired," I said, begging off. "Think I'll hang out in the Jacuzzi for a while and then watch a little TV and hit the sack."

"I'll stay with you," Donna offered.

One of the married men from our group was in the Jacuzzi when we arrived at the indoor pool area. "Just soaking my sore legs," he said, inviting us to join him. "I'm not used to so much walking."

Neither was I. The half an hour soak nicely loosened my aching joints. In that time, we heard about our companion's stint in the Korean War, as well as how he and his wife had met, the names of their kids and grandkids, and all the prescriptions he had to take for one ailment or another.

Once we were back in our room, Donna and I took turns showering and changed into our jammies. "Come here," she called, opening the sliding glass doors. We stood outside on our sixth floor balcony and watched a lightning storm electrify the distant mountains.

"Isn't that beautiful?" she cried.

"Magical. Are you glad you're here, Donna?"

"Oh, yes. We've had such fun already. I can't believe we have six days left. This was a good idea you had, Teresa." She hugged me, and I hadn't seen such a big smile on her face since Chad died.

"I saw you talking to Keith in the visitor center today," I ventured. "It looked like you were having a deep discussion."

Donna stared straight ahead with her hands on the balcony rail watching jagged streaks rhythmically light up the dark sky. "He's a kind man. What I said in my introduction on the bus touched him. He gave me some suggestions on how I can make some extra money to supplement my income."

The hairs on the back of my neck stood on end. "What kind of suggestions? Do you mean investments of some kind?"

"He just shared some ideas for someone like me who has trouble making ends meet. That's all."

I turned her toward me. "You don't know Keith," I reminded her. "Don't do anything stupid."

She rolled her eyes. "Give me a little credit, Teresa. I was Valedictorian of our senior class, in case you've forgotten."

"Yeah, well, that was a long time ago. People change."

She punched my arm light-heartedly. "Thanks, girlfriend!" She gasped when more lightning ricocheted across the mountains. Then she faced me again. "Don't worry, Teresa. I'm not stupid."

For some reason, I suddenly recalled the lyrics to that George Strait song, famous last words of a fool.

CHAPTER TEN
Be Careful What You Wish For

No one knows the real reason as to why I called off my first engagement. At the time, I'd cryptically told friends and family that I realized I didn't love Curt the way a woman should love a man. They were all heartbroken because everyone adored Curt. He was a good guy, and people told us we made the perfect pair. Everyone, that is, except my father, who I've already mentioned felt I was too stubborn and independent to commit to one man for a lifetime.

The truth was, Curt forgot my birthday. That's the reason I broke up with him. That year we were engaged, he completely forgot my birthday. No flowers, no present, not a card or even a greeting. To him, it was just another day.

It wasn't until I told him that my parents were taking us out for dinner to celebrate when it hit him. Of course, he profusely apologized and bent over backwards the *next* day to make me feel special. He showered me with the requisite presents: flowers, a box of candy that threatened to widen my hips, and a romantic card. But it was too late. As I lay in bed that night, I decided any man who couldn't remember his fiancée's birthday wouldn't remember his wife's, and that man didn't deserve me. I was confident in knowing my own needs and wants. I understood that Curt's tendency to space out on things I considered important would be a thorn in my side, and thorns hurt.

I never regretted my decision. A couple of years later, I heard Curt married a girl he met at a disco and they ended up moving down south somewhere, happy as two bugs in a rug.

Today was Sunday and Annette's birthday; the reason I'd recalled my birthday fiasco all those years ago. As far as I knew, Bruce hadn't called Annette since we'd left Illinois. Nor had her son, Dustin. I hoped the two of them would come through for her today of all days. But a sour feeling settled in the pit of my stomach.

Donna and I woke up Jackie and Kim, and the four of us stood in the hotel hallway in bare feet and jammies pounding on Annette and Crystal's door until it opened. "Happy birthday!" we shouted when Annette opened it. Smiling, her hair was styled perfectly, as if she'd been up for hours straight-ironing it. Crystal's short hair, on the other hand, was the epitome of bed head. She rubbed sleep from her eyes and yawned as we sang the happy birthday song to Annette. Then we all handed her our individual gifts, wrapped in pretty papers and ribbons.

"Thanks, girls. You're all so sweet."

"Today is the first day of the rest of your life," Kim said, stealing Annette's line.

"You may be fifty, but you don't look a day over forty-nine," Jackie joked, pinching a similar quote Chuck had used recently.

After a round of hugs, we retreated to our rooms to dress and prepare for the day ahead.

"How'd everyone sleep?" Keith asked when we were on the bus and passing by the Great Salt Lake, which looked like a mirage on the desert. He stood in front, as usual, looking surfer dude handsome while talking into his microphone.

"Great!" was the unified response.

For the first time in months, my body didn't ache. Maybe it was because we'd spent the night in the spiritually energized Salt Lake City. Or perhaps it had been the mattress in the hotel, which had felt like sleeping on a cloud.

"Today we're headed to Jackson Hole, Wyoming, by way of the Oregon Trail," Keith said. "We'll be spending the night in Jackson, and tomorrow, we'll visit the Grand Tetons before moving on to Yellowstone." His intense gaze zeroed in on Annette, pinning her to the back of her seat. "Today is a very special day," he announced. He offered Annette his hand. She accepted it, and he pulled her to her feet and flung his arm around her waist. Her face turned five shades of pink. "Today is Annette's birthday!" Keith exclaimed. "Happy birthday, Annette."

"Happy birthday!" everyone on the bus mimicked.

Keith squeezed Annette's waist a little tighter. "Wayne and I did some shopping last night, and today we'll be stopping at a park in Idaho Falls for a picnic lunch. We even managed to pick up a birthday cake. How about that, everyone?"

The people on the bus clapped, and Annette seemed overwhelmed. "Thank you, Keith and Wayne.

You're both so nice to have gone to the trouble."

"We normally don't need a reason to party on this tour," Wayne said, glancing over his shoulder and winking, "but a birthday gives us a legitimate excuse."

Annette returned to her seat smiling from ear to ear.

"Have you heard from Bruce and Dustin?" I asked from the seat behind her. Suddenly, her smile vanished, and I knew the answer. "Cell phone service is not good while on the road. The day's still young," I said, patting her shoulder.

"Right," she mumbled.

I had no idea why I was making excuses for those two. I'd be royally pissed if they disappointed her. My intuition told me to be prepared to add them to my *dog* list.

The drive through Idaho was beautiful with its wheat fields, majestic mountains, and herds of horses everywhere we looked. Wayne stopped in Idaho Falls at a pretty park filled with birdsong and the soothing sounds of a rippling creek. When he and Keith spread a lunch worthy of kings upon the picnic tables, we were impressed—and hungry.

"I wouldn't mind being fifty again," Joyce said, as we wolfed down sandwiches, potato salad, chips, and fresh fruit.

"What would you do differently if you had a do over?" I asked.

"I'd probably accept my boyfriend's proposal all those years ago. As it is, we've been together nineteen years and I don't see a reason to get married now."

"You've had a boyfriend for nineteen years?" Kim asked, almost choking on a pickle. Nine more years of living with Eddie without a marriage certificate and she'd be in the same boat.

"Yep," Joyce answered, shrugging. "It's worked out fine. He lives thirty miles away, so we're not under each other's feet all the time, and he can't boss me around! If he tries, he knows he won't be spending the night in my bed."

We laughed, and I gave Joyce a high five.

"At this age, it's better not to be married anyway, for tax purposes," she said.

I noticed Kim's gaze dipped to her lap. She suddenly seemed to have lost her appetite.

"Time for cake," Keith interrupted, carrying a store-bought, but personally decorated cake with Annette's name. He gingerly placed it on our picnic table. When he started singing the happy birthday song, everyone gathered around and joined in. I thought Annette might burst into tears. Wayne slipped a lighter from his pocket and set the few candles they'd stuck in the cake aflame.

"Make a wish and blow out the candles," Norma said.

Annette closed her eyes, made a wish, and blew. Everyone clapped.

"What'd you wish for?" Keith asked, sidling a little too close for comfort.

Their gazes connected. Something in her flirtatious tone alarmed me when she answered, "That's for me to know and you to find out."

CHAPTER ELEVEN
Million Dollar Birthday

By the time we reached Jackson, it was raining and fifty-six degrees.

"It's cold!" Crystal cried, wrapping her arms around herself as Keith and Wayne unloaded the luggage in front of the Antler Inn.

Jackie eyed the two-story log dwelling with suspicion. "This doesn't look like a four-star hotel."

"It's one block from the town square," Wayne said, "and steps from numerous restaurants, shops and art galleries. I think the inside will surprise you. The place is quite nice, even if there are actual elk antlers attached to the sign."

"The world-famous Million Dollar Cowboy Bar is also within rolling distance," Keith supplied.

Jackie turned her back on him, once again making me curious as what had happened between the two.

"I like it!" Annette said. "Looks rustic and completely charming. And I've heard of the cowboy bar. Can we go to it tonight?"

"You can do whatever you want while we're in Jackson," Keith said. "There's nothing planned as a group except dinner at a local restaurant."

"I've heard Harrison Ford and Calista Flockhart own a home here," Donna said.

Keith's muscles bulged as he lifted suitcases and travel bags from the coach and carried them to a spot under a protected awning. "They do, but don't hold your breath hoping to see them. They're private people."

I was searching through the sea of luggage for my bags when I saw Keith subtly motion to Donna with his finger. She stepped to him and he whispered something in her ear. Nonchalantly trying to eavesdrop was of no use. Their voices were low. The only words I caught were "finalize tonight" from him and "after dinner" from her.

When she and I unloaded our stuff into our room and freshened up, I wanted so bad to ask her what that conversation had been about. But she'd already warned me in that sweet way of hers to butt out. Instead, I commented on how clean the room was and how I liked the headboards that were made of twisted tree branches.

Luckily, all six of us had packed umbrellas, because it was still raining when we gathered to trek to the town square to check out the quaint shops. We hit almost every shop. Everything was too expensive for my wallet, but I splurged and bought a sweatshirt with *Jackson Hole, Wyoming* printed on the front since I hadn't packed anything warm and I was freezing. The other girls bought at least one souvenir, with the exception of Jackie who juggled six bags of new clothes in her hands three hours later.

"Look at those arches formed out of elk antlers." Donna pointed to the gigantic arches on the corners of the town square. The rain had finally stopped, and we were able to enjoy the authentic western town and its outdoor attractions.

"Anyone want to take a ride on the stagecoach?" I asked, noting a stage stop and an authentic red U.S. mail coach being driven by horses.

"I'd rather go see the cowboy bar," Annette said.

"Whatever you want," Kim replied. "It's your birthday."

Inside the nondescript wooden façade with the neon sign was a saloon that displayed the true atmosphere of the Wild West. Red carpet, cowboy memorabilia and murals, knobbled pine architecture, and barstools made of genuine leather saddles greeted us when we stepped into the dim interior. A stage for bands or dancing was at the far end of the building. Four guys in cowboy hats and baseball caps played at one of the pool tables. Only a few other customers lined the bar at that time of day.

"What'll you have, ladies?" the bartender asked us. We all ordered a beer, except for Annette, who was a strict teetotaler.

"I'll have a Coke," she said, running her palm across the long polished bar.

"This bar is embellished with five hundred and ninety-two silver dollars," the bartender said. He pointed to the coins embedded in the wood.

"Do you have live music?" Kim asked.

"Do we ever. Some of the best country musicians have played here. Waylon Jennings, Glen Campbell, Tanya Tucker, Hoyt Axton, Willie Nelson... You name them, they've played here." He set glasses of beer and Coke in front of us. "You ladies ought to come back tonight. There's no live band on Sunday nights, but we'll have jukebox music and you can dance to your heart's desire."

He'd mentioned the magic word. "We're line dancers," Jackie told him. "Maybe we'll perform for your customers tonight, if you promise to pour us a free round of drinks."

The bartender grinned, displaying a gap between his front teeth. "My customers would enjoy a live performance by such a comely group of ladies. It's a promise."

"I like this place," Annette said, gazing around.

"It's her birthday today," Crystal told the bartender.

"Happy birthday, ma'am. That Coke is on the house. You all stop by later tonight and we'll help you celebrate. Won't we, boys?" He glanced at the men playing pool. One of them mumbled, "Hell, yeah."

"We will. Thank you," Annette replied with a smile.

~ * ~

During dinner, Annette invited everyone from our tour to join us at the Million Dollar Cowboy Bar at nine o'clock to see us dance and to celebrate her birthday. Some of the more adventurous seniors accepted the invitation, including the five amigas. By the time nine o'clock arrived, however, only three women were still gung ho to accompany us.

The neon sign outside the bar was lit up when we arrived, and a dozen motorcycles were parked along the street.

"Do you think there might be a rumble tonight?" Doris asked, causing us to chuckle. She and her daring friends followed us inside.

The place was jam-packed and jumping with music, people playing pool, and raucous chatter. The same bartender from the afternoon waved to us when he saw us.

"I was hoping you ladies meant it when you said you'd be back tonight. As you can see, we have a full crowd waiting to watch you dance."

"Where'd they all come from?" Donna asked, glancing around at the bikers, cowboys, and a couple of men who looked like fish out of water in their suits and ties.

"Jackson is a small town, ma'am. Word gets around fast, especially when pretty ladies are involved."

"I'm nervous," Crystal admitted, glimpsing at the roughnecks lining the bar. "What if they don't like us and boo us off the stage?"

Jackie rolled her eyes. "That's not going to happen. Most of these guys are already drunk from the looks of it. They'd probably whistle at dogs dressed in tutus."

"Are you comparing us to dogs?" Crystal said, planting her hands on her wide hips.

"Please stop fussing with each other," Annette said. "I want to have a drink and then dance." She gently squeezed her way between two men sitting at the bar and flashed them her best beauty pageant smile. "Excuse me, gentlemen. It's my birthday today and I'd like a drink. Please pour me a glass of wine, bartender."

"Coming up, little lady. Would you like Chardonnay or Merlot?"

"Surprise me."

"One of your golden ales for the rest of us," Jackie said. "And remember your promise about a free round."

No one seemed surprised or concerned that Annette was drinking alcohol except me. In a lifetime of knowing her, I'd never seen her drink, not even on New Year's Eve. In Vegas, she'd left the strawberry daiquiri ordered by the amigas sit untouched. Her father had died of alcoholism when she was twelve, and she'd always been afraid the disease was hereditary, so she stayed away from it. I watched closely as she downed the glass of Merlot the bartender placed in front of her.

"Another one, please," she said, licking her lips. "That stuff is good."

The bartender handed her another glass, and she gulped it like a goldfish. I nearly toppled a man off his stool shoving my way next to her. "Annette, don't you think you ought to slow down? You've never had wine before. You don't know how it'll affect you."

"Affect me? I'm fifty and I feel wonderful, Teresa! Don't I look wonderful?" she asked the man on one side of her.

"You look good enough to eat." His wolfish expression scared even me. When he slapped Annette on the butt and she squealed, I grabbed her arm and pulled her away from the bar. "Time to dance," I said.

"Oh, goodie." She clapped her hands like a baby.

"Is she drunk already?" Jackie asked me, as the six of us moved toward the stage. Annette wobbled some.

"I think so. It doesn't take much for a non-drinker. I just hope she doesn't throw up. Kim, will you find us a good song on the jukebox?"

As soon as we lined up on the stage, the crowd cheered and clapped. I couldn't help but smile. There we were, six broads almost fifty years old from an itty-bitty town in the Midwest about to dance in one of the most famous bars in the modern west. It was surreal. I looked up into the sea of faces, just as Brooks and Dunn's *Boot Scootin' Boogie* started blasting from the jukebox.

We all knew that dance so well we could have done it in our sleep. None of us made a misstep, not even Annette, tipsy as she was. When our performance was over, all hell broke loose. The men whooped and whistled and demanded an encore. We happily obliged and then took our final bows. To wild applause, we left the stage and pushed through the crowd of rowdy men while making our way to a table in the front of the room. When I looked for our senior friends, it appeared they'd left. I doubted it was their kind of scene. I wasn't even sure it was my kind.

"Nice job, ladies," the bartender said, delivering a tray of drinks to us. "Beers on the house for you five and another Merlot for the birthday girl."

I frowned. "Wouldn't you rather have a Coke?" I asked Annette.

"She's only turning fifty once in her life," Jackie said, smacking my hand. "Let her have some fun. God knows she never has a moment of pleasure except for when she's with us. Bruce and Dustin have all but crushed her spirit."

"Damn men," Annette slurred. "They didn't even call to wish me a happy birthday."

Before I could get a word in edgewise, Annette sucked down the wine like it was a Slurpee drink. Suddenly, Keith appeared at the table, halting our conversation. Smelling fresh and soapy, his blond hair was still damp, like he'd just stepped out of the shower. Wisps fell across his forehead and over his eyes in a sexy way. I hated to admit it, but he looked pretty hot in a blue chambray shirt, tight jeans and cowboy boots. Despite his looks, or maybe *because* of them, he made me nervous.

Crystal's eyes lit up. "Keith! Won't you join us?"

His carefree gaze flitted around the table. "Don't mind if I do." He pulled out a chair next to Annette, flipped it around, and straddled it.

"Too bad you weren't here a few minutes earlier," Crystal said. "You just missed our show."

"Dang it. That's the reason I came."

"Maybe another time," Kim said, sipping her beer.

I noticed Jackie's gaze was stuck to the glass cradled in her hands. When Keith nodded at Donna in a knowing way, she smiled. Crystal's cheeks flamed when he winked at her. None of us seemed immune to his charms, except me. For some reason, I wasn't a woman he paid particular attention to.

"Looks like you're having a good time," he said to Annette, snuggling close to her shoulder.

"Oh, yes. This is the best birthday ever." She giggled like a love-struck teenager.

Jackie unexpectedly bolted up from her chair.

"I'm going back to the motel."

"Wait. You can't walk back by yourself in the dark," I said.

"Then come with me if you want. Either way, I'm leaving now." Her mouth pressed into a fine line, and she shot daggers at Keith and pushed away from the table and marched toward the door.

"Hold on, Jackie!" Torn between staying to watch over Annette and walking back to the Antler Inn with Jackie, I glanced around the table wishing that someone else, for once, would take charge.

"Go with her." Kim nudged my arm. "We'll finish our drinks and be back soon. I think birthday girl has had about enough partying for one night, anyway."

"All right. Thanks." I nodded to Kim and kissed Annette on the cheek. "Happy birthday, honey. See you back in the room, Donna."

Keith grabbed my wrist as I walked by him. "Don't worry, Teresa. I'll make sure Annette's taken care of and everyone returns to the motel safely."

Little did I know then what his idea of taking care of Annette meant.

CHAPTER TWELVE
Mama Bear

"Where's Annette?" I asked Crystal the next morning. Donna and I pulled out some chairs and joined her, Jackie, and Kim at their table for breakfast at the Teton Steakhouse. They all had mugs of coffee and half-eaten plates of food in front of them.

"She'd just gotten up when I left the room and didn't look so good. I think she'll have a pretty bad hangover today."

Everyone but me chuckled. "I was out like a light the moment my head hit the pillow. What time did you all get back to the motel?"

"The four of us got in around ten thirty," Crystal said. "I'm not sure about Annette. I was exhausted and went right to sleep. Traveling and socializing all day zaps my energy. Plus, the night sweats are keeping me up at night. That natural remedy I'm taking isn't worth crap."

My head tilted, but it wasn't Crystal's menopausal symptoms that caused me concern. "What do you mean you don't know about Annette? Didn't she walk back with you from the bar?"

Donna absently moved sausage around her plate

with a fork. "Keith bought her one more birthday drink as we were leaving and said he'd escort her to the motel."

The blood in my veins caught fire and sizzled. "You weren't supposed to leave her alone," I hissed. Close to exploding, it took all my effort to keep my voice low so as not to attract attention from the other patrons.

"She wasn't alone," Kim reminded me. "Keith said he'd take care of her."

My clenched fist banged the table. When a few people looked our way, I smiled and said, "Good morning" and unrolled my hand. Then my angry gaze raked over my friends. "I can't believe you left her in the hands of a stranger, and drunk for the first time, too. Great friends you are." I stood up, disgusted. "I'm going to check on her and make sure she's all right."

Kim stopped me with a hand on my arm. "She's okay, Teresa. Just a little hung over. That's all. What are you getting so worked up about, anyway? Annette's a grown woman. Stop treating her like she's a child."

I inhaled a deep breath and plopped back into my chair. "You're right, but she was vulnerable last night. As far as I know, that ass, Bruce, hasn't called her since we left Illinois. Women can do stupid things when they're upset and hurting, and drunk. Or when they feel they have something to prove." I glanced at Jackie, who hadn't yet commented. "Do you agree, Jackie?"

She shrugged her shoulders and slipped the sunglasses from on top of her head to cover her slightly puffy eyes.

"Stop worrying and eat something, Mama Bear," Crystal advised. She pushed her plate of leftover eggs toward me. "Annette will meet us on the bus, and you'll see she's okay.

~ * ~

Annette was the last to board the coach. I was just about to go looking for her when she scurried past Keith without a passing glance and slid onto the seat next to Crystal. I couldn't help but emit a small gasp. My friend was as pale as a ghost and her hands shook with a noticeable tremor.

Keith's usual bright smile and cheerful voice came over the speakers, stopping me from darting across the aisle to ask if she felt all right. "We are *not* letting her drink again," I whispered to my seatmate, Jackie.

"Good morning, folks!" Keith exclaimed.

"Good morning!"

Wayne maneuvered the bus out of the parking lot as Keith began his morning speech. "We have a full schedule today. Our first stop will be at the Grand Teton National Park visitor center for a little history, and where you'll gaze upon the magnificent Grand Tetons and Snake River. After that, we'll take you to a lovely little chapel called the Chapel of the Transfiguration. This was an Episcopal chapel built of logs in 1925 for ranchers in the isolated area to attend. Wayne and I have brought our last two tours there. People have really enjoyed the serenity of the area and the aspen groves surrounding it. Chances are, you'll see pronghorn antelope, elk and deer springing through the meadows. Those are some great photo ops. Then we're headed to Jenny Lake and Mount Moran, named after Thomas Moran, an artist who painted landscapes of the area. After a shopping stop, we're on to beautiful Colter Bay, where we'll enjoy a picnic lunch by the water. And that's just the first half of our day!"

Although a tiny spark still burned under my skin for the way my friends had abandoned Annette the night before, I decided to stop acting like a mother hen and enjoy the day. After all, despite looking like death warmed over, she'd survived her birthday bash.

The morning was as spectacular as Keith had promised. I'd never seen such awesome beauty in my life and doubted I ever would again. The weather was perfect, as well.

As we ate our lunch on the banks of the amazingly beautiful Colter Bay, everyone was eager to share their favorite moments from that morning. Those of us who could get up and down without too many bones crackling and popping found spots on the grass while the majority of the group sat at picnic tables.

"I snapped a few good photos of some yellow-headed blackbirds who posed for us," Bill said. He and Violet sat at one of the tables with her sister, Daisy, and Chuck.

"Wayne told us ringing the bell in that little chapel will bring good luck. I hope he's right," Daisy said. "At my age, I can use all the luck I can get."

Chuck wiggled his eyebrows at her. "You've met me, Daisy. I'd say your luck has already changed for the better."

"What about those trumpeter swans and white pelicans at Oxbow Bend?" Barb said from another table. "Weren't they pretty?"

"What is that white flower I keep seeing all over the place?" Joyce inquired.

"Keith said it's called common yarrow," Winnie told her. "Did I show you the art I bought in the souvenir shop, Joyce? The artist is a Navajo, and he was actually there to sign the print. He told me he draws with colored pencils on ledger paper because that was the first type of paper the Indians received from the white man long ago."

I smiled at the chatter going on around me and hoped I'd be healthy enough to take another trip like this when I was the age of my fellow travelers. Lying back in the fresh grass, I closed my eyes and savored the warm sun on my face and skin, thankful to be sharing the experience with my best friends.

Kim wasn't far from me, also sitting on the grass. As I lay there thinking it would be so easy to nod off and take a quick nap, I heard the soft shuffle of feet and then Keith's voice. My eyes remained closed, but my ears perked.

"Did you find anything interesting in the souvenir shop, Kim?" he asked quietly. When she didn't answer, he said, "Maybe you found something interesting at the gift store when we were in Bryce Canyon. Did you happen to pick anything up there?"

When there was still no response from Kim, I opened my eyes and slowly turned my head in that direction. Kim's mouth hung open, and her eyes were as wide as saucers.

"Cat got your tongue?" Keith asked, quirking that familiar grin.

My stomach rolled like a wave. The questions

may have seemed innocent to someone less observant than me, but I sensed the threat in Keith's tone and saw intimidation in his eyes. Why was he so interested in what she'd bought as souvenirs? And why did Kim look like she might faint? Or puke?

"Leave me alone, Keith," she said softly.

He chuckled and walked away, not realizing I'd been watching and listening.

I sat up. "What was that about?" I asked Kim when he was out of earshot.

"Nothing." She uncrossed her legs and stood up and stretched her back.

"It sounded like something to me. Something weird."

"He was flirting. That's all. Haven't you noticed? He's hitting on everyone under seventy on the bus."

"He hasn't hit on me," I said, feigning disappointment.

"That's because you give off that vibe."

"What vibe?"

"That you aren't interested. You don't flirt, even unconsciously. By the way, have you contacted Phil since we've been away?"

I sighed. "Do you *all* know about me and Phil?"

"Of course we do, Teresa. You can't hide your sexy business from your best friends."

"So I've been told."

She helped me up from the ground. I noticed everyone packing up and heading toward the parking lot.

"How's Eddie?" I asked. I didn't care for the man, but I suddenly felt like she needed me to acknowledge him. And I wanted to take the subject off of Phil and me.

She shrugged her shoulders. "You know Eddie. Nothing much changes with him. But at least he converses with me. That's more than I can say for Bruce. Poor Annette. Do you know she takes anxiety medicine because of him? He makes her life hell."

I was worried about Annette, especially since she'd acted depressed all day, but I had no intention of letting Kim change the topic. It was her I was thinking about at that moment. "Maybe you can take some time on this vacation to consider what or who *you* really want in your life, Kim. It's not too late to make decisions that will make you happy."

Her brows drew together. "Who says I'm unhappy?"

"I do. You've been acting different lately. I've seen a change in you, and it started around New Year's Eve. What are you hiding?" I was tired of beating around the bush.

Her nostrils flared and she chewed her lower lip, probably to keep from biting my head off. "Looks like it's about time to get back on the bus," she snapped.

With that, she strode away, bringing our conversation to a screeching halt.

CHAPTER THIRTEEN
Bison, Elk and Bears, Oh My!

In 1988, 793,000 acres of Yellowstone National Park burned. It was the largest wildfire in recorded history of the park and lasted two months before the arrival of cool and moist weather in late autumn brought the fires to an end. That was only one of the many tidbits of interesting information Keith showered us with as Wayne entered the park early that afternoon and drove us past stands of dead lodgepole pines.

"The park is also home to diverse wildlife, including grizzly bears, wolves, bison and elk," he said. His head turned, and he pointed out the window to a lone bison sauntering slowly down the road next to us. Those of us sitting next to windows plastered our faces to the glass while people from the opposite aisles moved to our side to catch a glimpse of the elderly beast.

"That bull was probably forced out of the herd due to his age," Keith said.

"Poor thing. It's the same as sticking us elderly in nursing homes," Doris grumbled.

"Unfortunately, in nature, it's survival of the fittest," Keith responded with a sympathetic smile.

"But you shouldn't worry, Doris." He grinned. "You're still fit as a fiddle."

Despite my suspicions that Keith was a playboy of the worst kind, there was no concrete evidence (as of yet) with which to support my theory, except that neither Annette nor Jackie would look him in the eye. Player or not, he was one heck of a tour director. His broad historical knowledge on all the places we visited was extraordinary. And his wit, charm, and enthusiasm made for a fun atmosphere, as evidenced by the fuzzy hat with plastic horns and buffalo face he wore that day. Attending to the need of every one of the travelers seemed to be his specialty. The older women adored him. The men wished they still had his looks and vitality.

His effect on my friends was a little different, and that worried me. Slowly and steadily, I began to believe that Keith symbolized the youth and dreams we were leaving behind as we turned half a century old. Instead of him inspiring my gal pals to embrace their vibrant and beautiful lives as mature women, he seemed to have a way of zeroing in on their weaknesses and taking advantage.

At the time, I couldn't quite put my finger on it. Looking back, I see clearly that the man was a master at manipulation. He gave each woman what she wanted or needed at the precise moment she wanted or needed it. Like a spider, he used a variety of strategies to attract and capture his prey. Then he trapped his prey in a sick, sticky web of deceit. I had a sinking feeling that three of my friends had already gotten stuck in that web, and I didn't know how to un-stick them.

Our first stop in Yellowstone was the West Thumb Geyser Basin. Wooden boardwalks made walking and viewing the geysers, hot springs, and mud pots easy. According to a pamphlet we were given, varying water temperatures and bacteria caused the different colors. Some of the names of the volcanic pools were a mystery to me. For instance, the Black Pool was actually a vibrant turquoise color, and the mud volcanoes were white and looked like foam. All of the springs were beautiful, and it felt like we were on another planet.

There finally came a moment when I was able to get Annette alone and interrogate her. "Are you feeling all right? You haven't been yourself today. Not once have I seen you smile. Are you still sick from last night?"

"I'm sick, all right," she whispered, not meeting my gaze.

I made her face me and lifted her chin up with my finger. "What is it, Annette? You can tell me. I'll help if I can." I placed my hand on her shoulders in a gesture of support and comfort, but she wriggled out of my grasp.

"I'm an idiot, but I've only myself to blame," she hissed.

Assuming she was talking about getting drunk last night, I cocked a faint smile. "Don't be so hard on yourself. It was your fiftieth birthday. It's okay you went a little berserk. God knows you never let your hair down. So you got a little drunk. Big deal."

Her lips pursed and she struggled to hold back tears. "I did more than let my hair down, Teresa."

"What'd you do?" Although the sun was beating

down on my skin, my body temperature dropped. Suddenly, I felt very cold.

Annette squeezed her eyes shut. Then she said, "I don't want to talk about it. Please don't ask me any more questions." And she walked away.

Three hours later, Keith gathered the group around the bus. "Since the day is late, we'll see more of the park tomorrow, including the Lower waterfalls and the famous Old Faithful geyser and Inn. Right now, we'll head over to Grant Village Lodge, our hotel for the night. Grant Village is popular with tourists because the lodge is the only accommodations inside the park."

On our way there, the bus erupted with excitement when Wayne stopped alongside the road and pointed out a herd of buffalo in the distance. They were grazing beside a creek. It felt like we'd traveled back in history to a time when buffalo roamed the prairies by the thousands. He told us bison can sprint at thirty miles per hour, and many visitors have gotten too close and been gored.

Crystal stood up and snapped pictures through the window. "I'm so glad we got to see a real herd! I was afraid the only one we'd encounter was the stuffed buffalo in front of that shop in Jackson."

She was still peering through the glass as she lowered her weight into her seat when Keith tossed a Whoopee cushion onto it. Everyone laughed, of course, when the sound exploded under her fanny.

"Very funny, Keith." She wagged her finger at him like he was a bad boy. When he reached out for the toy, she shook her head and tucked it into her shoulder bag. "This is mine now. You like jokes, huh?

When you least expect it, I'll get you back."

That was the first prank he pulled on Crystal, but it wouldn't be the last.

~ * ~

The lodge was actually a group of buildings into which we were all divided. The buildings themselves and the dormitory-style rooms inside were old and outdated. Keith had warned us ahead of time there would be no televisions, radios, or mini fridges in the rooms, as well as no cell phone service or internet availability. Atmosphere and location inside the park, however, made the lack of conveniences worth it—so he said.

When Donna and I dragged our luggage from the bus to our building, an elk was on the footpath eating grass!

"Now that's something you don't see every day," I said, making a large arc around the elk and hoping he wouldn't attack.

"He must be used to people," Donna said, strolling past the animal without a care.

Our room with its two twin beds was small, clean and functional, even if it lacked charm and character. Because of the isolated area, I was happy for hot water to shower with and a restaurant beside the lake that served a decent meal.

Later, after we'd returned from dinner, Donna and I organized our clothes in our suitcases, painted our nails, and wrote in our journals. There were no activities planned for the tour group together and nothing to do in Grant Village. There wasn't even a pool table in the lobby of the building. At dinner, Jackie, Kim, Crystal and Annette had said they were going to stay in their rooms for the evening and go to bed early.

Restless, I paced our room. Donna was scooted up against her headboard sketching a picture of a buffalo on her sketchpad. I peeked at the drawing and gave her a thumbs-up.

"You're such a good artist. Why haven't you ever sold your work?"

Her hand stilled, and she looked at me as if I'd grown two heads. "Are you crazy? No one would want to buy my sketches."

I plopped on the end of her bed. "Of course people would! You're talented. I wish you wouldn't sell yourself short. Didn't you win some art awards and contests when we were in high school?"

"Yeah, but that was a long time ago. I just draw for fun these days."

An idea struck me. "Wouldn't it be neat if you could market your drawings to companies that sell stuff like calendars, magnets, greeting cards, totes, and tee shirts? It could be the start of a brand new career, or a way for you to earn extra money. You've said you need to supplement your income. Annette's husband is a businessman. Maybe he could give you some tips on how to break into that kind of field."

Donna's head snapped up. "Get real, Teresa. It's a little late for a new career. Besides, I already have a plan for supplementing my income, thanks to Keith."

Finally! It was about time she explained. "Keith? Is that what you've been talking to him about?"

She hid a smile. "Forget I said anything. I'll tell

you more by the end of the week when I have further details. Suffice it to say, he's helping me to improve my financial life."

"How?" I demanded. "He's a tour guide. What does he know about finances?"

"Be patient and I'll tell you all about it when the time is right." She continued drawing. "He's a lot more savvy that you might imagine."

My gaze narrowed. "You haven't fallen in love with Keith and done something asinine, have you?"

Her laughter filled the small room. "No, I'm not in love with Keith. And I don't see how improving one's lot in life can be asinine. Now go read your Kindle and let me finish this sketch before the natural light is gone, will you?"

Frustrated with Donna's secrecy, I stretched out on my bed and turned on my Kindle. I'd downloaded several books before coming on the trip, but I could no more focus on reading than I could do a headstand. The conversation with her made my head spin wondering what kind of cahoots she was in with Keith. I also worried about what Kim was hiding, and I didn't understand Jackie and Annette's sudden change in behavior.

"I need some fresh air. I'm going for a walk to the lake," I said, stuffing my Kindle into its case and grabbing my Jackson Hole sweatshirt from my suitcase.

"Okay, but don't stay out long. It'll be dark soon, and there might be bears around. We're in the wilderness, you know. Remember the elk on the sidewalk?"

"I'll be careful and take a flashlight and Mace

with me." I pulled the sweatshirt over my head and looped my mini flashlight around my wrist. Then I removed the bottle of Mace I carried in my purse at all times and stuck it in my jeans pocket.

"Mace won't take down a grizzly," Donna noted, as I closed the door behind me.

I had so much pent-up energy and adrenaline flowing through me, I figured I could take down a bear with my bare hands if need be. When I got to the lake, the sun was about to set and the temperature fell quickly. Glad to be wearing the sweatshirt and jeans, I walked along the shore, surprised there was no one else out and about.

The sun melting into the horizon was beautiful, but the lonesome squawks of birds and the soft splash of the water upon the beach reminded me of the moment in a horror movie when someone was about to be snuck up on and slashed to death. Spooked, I thought maybe it hadn't been a good idea for me to take a walk alone.

When I heard footsteps behind me, my heart pounded with an insane rhythm, and a scream caught silently in my throat. I jammed my hand into my pocket and withdrew the Mace. The only thing worse than being clawed to death by a bear was to be physically assaulted. What an idiot I was to go out there alone!

Whirling, I raised the Mace to eye level and put my finger on the trigger, ready to blind my pursuer and run.

"Stop! Don't shoot!" the man shouted, raising his arms in surrender. "I'm unarmed."

I squinted, recognizing the voice. "Keith? Is that

you?"

His arms swung to his sides and he stepped closer. "I'm sorry to have scared you, Teresa. I should have called out your name instead of sneaking up on you like that."

With a trembling hand, I lowered the Mace. "Yeah, you should have. You almost got a face full of chemicals." I snorted out short breaths in an attempt to settle my nerves. "What are you doing out here, anyway?"

"Just getting a little exercise while clearing my head. It's a quiet spot in which to think." The cords on his neck flexed and quivered. "What about you?"

"The same thing. There's nothing to do around here."

He grinned. "Most people enjoy the peace and solitude of being surrounded by nature."

"I enjoy it, too. There's a lot on my mind tonight, that's all, and I could use a distraction."

Our gazes latched, and a vague sense of unease snuck along my chest wall. His mouth opened as if he was about to offer a suggestion and then it snapped shut like a trap door. The breeze off the lake blew a few strands of his wispy hair into his eyes. I couldn't imagine a better looking man as the blush of moonlight touched his face. But that didn't mean I wasn't onto him. I worried that Annette's near confession earlier in the day had to do with him. For that reason alone, I was leery.

I was about to ask him straight out if he'd hurt her in some way when he seemed to read my mind and diverted the subject. "I'll be glad to walk you to your building. It's not a good idea to be out here alone, especially at night. There are a lot of wild creatures on the prowl."

I'll bet," I thought. *Are you one of them?* Accepting his offer, because I couldn't come up with an excuse not to, we walked along the shoreline and back to the building in silence. "Thanks," I said outside the main door. "See you in the morning."

"Good night, Teresa." He tipped his head as any gentleman would and disappeared into the dark before I could blurt out the questions that lingered on the tip of my tongue. I stood in the dark wondering why he hadn't flirted or tried to hit on me. I wasn't sure whether I should be relieved or insulted.

Maybe I *did* give off a vibe, as Kim had suggested. If that were the case, I had no problem with that. An icy feeling slid up my arms. Keith was trouble with a capital T, and it wouldn't be long before the truth came out. Of that I was sure.

CHAPTER FOURTEEN
Fun and Games?

Our group sat on benches in the viewing area near Old Faithful waiting for it to erupt. So far it had been thirty minutes with no sign of a sputter. Apparently, it erupted every ninety-two minutes without fail, and Keith and Wayne had timed our visit so that we'd experience the big show in about five more minutes.

"Unfortunately, most of my recent boyfriends have taken the same amount of time to go off," Doris joked, sending all of us into fits of laughter.

A few minutes later, Crystal expelled a blood-curdling scream a few seats down from me. She shot up from the bench and ran into the grass. I thought a swarm of bees had attacked. Upon closer inspection, I discovered Keith had thrown a rubber snake into her lap.

The seniors chuckled and thought his joking around was funny. Crystal didn't seem to mind either, once she realized the snake was a fake. She winged it back at him and would have chucked him in the head if he hadn't ducked.

"You're really asking for it today," she warned in a teasing voice.

"Asking for what?" he joked back.

"Keep messing with me and you'll find out."

The pranks that had started yesterday continued in full swing today. Earlier that morning, after enjoying Artist Point (the Grand Canyon of the Yellowstone) and posing for photos in front of the incredible Lower Falls, Keith asked Crystal if she'd buy him a beer that night if he hit the sign across the road with a rock on the first try. "Sure," she said. Then he ran across the road and struck the sign with the rock.

"You owe me a beer tonight. You can pay up at the bowling alley in Billings," he said after he'd jogged back.

"You're a cheater." She playfully smacked his arm. He bumped hips with her, causing her to yelp and lose her balance. Fortunately, he caught her in his arms before she fell. She laughed, clearing enjoying the attention. But when her gaze clouded with a mixture of admiration and lust, a chill like the brush of cobwebs crept up my arms.

"There she blows," Wayne hollered. I jerked my gaze away from Crystal and Keith and began snapping the requisite photos. A cloud of steam exploded from the most recognizable geyser in the world, eliciting gasps all around me. It took all of fifteen seconds for the billowing column to reach a height of 130 feet, before rapidly lowering after about twenty seconds. The big production ended with a few puffs of steam before disappearing back into the earth.

"That was a little disappointing," I said to Winnie and Barb, who sat on either side of me. "Guess I was expecting more."

"Me, too. To think I've been waiting all my life to

see Old Faithful, and it was over in twenty seconds." Winnie shook her head, looking disgusted.

"Let's go to the Inn and do some retail shopping," Barb suggested, looping her arm through Winnie's. "Buying crap I don't need always makes me feel better after a disappointment."

I walked with them to the Old Faithful Inn and bought myself a Yellowstone tee shirt, a coffee mug, another postcard for my scrapbook, and a second card for Phil. Turned out, spending money made me feel better, too.

~ * ~

Back on the bus, we watched a video on Custer's Last Stand and then played a trivia game on our way to the historic cattle town of Billings, Montana. The game was a quiz on the Tetons, and one of the married men tied for first place with Crystal.

"I've written down a number," Keith said. "Pick a number between one and one hundred. Whomever is closest wins this bar of soap shaped like a Yellowstone bear cub." He held up the green soap so everyone could see how cute it was. "Crystal, you go first."

"Oh, I want that soap!" she squealed. "My lucky number is four. I hope it's four. I hope it's four."

"Tom?"

"My lucky number is twenty-seven."

Keith withdrew the slip of paper from behind his back but didn't show us what he'd written on it. "The number is ten. Crystal, you win!" I wondered if he'd let her win.

She rocketed up from her seat and reached

between my head and Kim's to grab for the soap. "Thank you, Keith. I've never won anything before."

"You're welcome, Crystal," he winked. He stared at her a minute. "Hey, I have an idea. I'm supposed to tell the group some things about Deadwood, South Dakota now, but my throat is a little scratchy. Do you want to take over my job for a while?"

"Me?" Her eyes bulged.

He grinned brightly and motioned her up front. "Come on, it'll be fun. I have a feeling you're a natural."

"Okay," she giggled.

Keith slid onto the seat directly behind Wayne and patted the spot next to him. "Sit next to me, Crystal." When she did, he handed her a big three-ring binder. "Just read this stuff into the microphone. If you feel creative, you can throw in a few jokes."

"I only know knock-knock jokes," she said. "But I was in the class play when we were high school seniors. I suppose I could dramatize a bit as I read."

"Perfect. I knew I'd made the right choice when I picked you."

My eyes narrowed into slits. *Snagged in your web, you mean*, I thought uncharitably.

Everyone," he announced into the microphone, "please make your new tour director, or rather, your tour director for the next fifteen minutes, feel welcome." When he turned the microphone over to Crystal, everyone clapped. He squeezed her shoulder and then laid his head back on the seat to rest.

Crystal did a great job as substitute tour director. She made people laugh whether she intended to or not. Keith, who had most of the women on the tour wrapped around his finger, earned himself more Brownie points.

"Wasn't that nice of Keith to let Crystal have the spotlight?" I heard Joyce say from the other side of the coach. "I think it made her feel special."

Hmmph! My friend was already a special person. She didn't need the likes of him to make her feel special. The way he'd been giving her attention all day, I couldn't help but wonder what he wanted from Crystal. That niggling feeling twanged my nerves.

Our accommodations for the night were at the Sheraton in Billings. Keith had told us that although Billings was the largest city in Montana, there was no nightlife to speak of. However, there was a bowling alley. Hearing that news got my blood pumping. Crystal and I had been on the bowling team in high school, and we'd joined a couple of leagues as adults.

"We're gonna smoke our friends and anyone else who's up for a challenge," I told her with confidence.

That evening as the games were about to begin, Keith nudged Crystal's arm. "Remember, you owe me a beer."

She smiled. "I haven't forgotten, and I always pay my debts. Be right back." Off she went to the snack bar. I watched her out of the corner of my eye while lacing up pathetically old red and blue bowling shoes. When she returned, she handed Keith a tall glass of foaming root beer. "You didn't say what kind of beer," she teased. "Two can play that game."

"Yes!" I chuckled. "Way to get him." Our palms smacked together in a high five.

He guzzled down the root beer and then removed his own personal bowling ball from a bag with his name stitched on it. "Last time I bowled, my score was two hundred," he said, inflating his chest like a rooster.

He had no idea how competitive Crystal and I could be when it came to bowling. We were beasts on the lanes! It took all my willpower not to pound on my chest like an ape at his comment. "Crystal and I were on the bowling team in high school, and we won the national championship when we were seniors," I told him, proudly. "Crystal was our anchor. Do you know what that means?"

"Yes, I do," he smiled. "It means she was a pretty good bowler. *Was* being the operative word here. It's been a while since you ladies were in high school. No offense." Grinning like a hyena, he slipped on his own personal shoes.

"No offense taken," Crystal said, popping her fingers in the bowling ball holes to limber them up, like she did back in the day.

"Bowling is like riding a bike," I said. "You never forget how. We were both good at the sport then, and we still are. Care to make a wager on which of us wins tonight, Keith? We'll average two games and the one with the best score will be the winner."

"I'm betting on Crystal or Teresa," Bill said. He and Chuck and their lady friends had gathered around us, as had the other handful of travelers who had come out for a night of fun.

"Me, too," Chuck said. "They look pumped up and ready to go."

"Thanks for your support, gentlemen." Keith feigned disappointment, and we all laughed. He reached out to shake our hands. "You're on, ladies. May the best bowler win."

Two games later, Crystal had not only beaten me *and* Keith, she'd also bowled a turkey in each round to boot. He took the loss as we all expected—with a grin and a suggestive wink. "Come with me, Crystal, and I'll give you your prize."

CHAPTER FIFTEEN
From A Seed...

Fiery, feisty, quick tempered, unpredictable and passionate: just some of the labels attached to redheads. Are they justified? In my case, the answer would be yes.

There were plenty of occasions when I was growing up that I'd burst into a rage, only to calm down and think: "Where did that come from?" As for the times I fell in love too fast, I usually blamed my hair color on the ardor and obsession that followed.

There have definitely been moments throughout my life when my impulses have gotten the best of me and caused a few problems. I had to admit, in times like those, it is quite useful to be able to say something like: "Well, what do you expect? I'm a redhead."

That excuse was about to come into play again very soon.

The next morning, I sat on the bus headed for South Dakota and Little Bighorn, sliding a glance toward Crystal, who slumped in the seat across the aisle from me. Last night at the bowling alley, after the games were over and we were all removing our shoes and putting away our balls, she'd disappeared for about fifteen minutes. So had Keith. When she reappeared from the vicinity of the bathrooms looking flushed and dreamy-eyed, I made her tell me what she'd been up to. I had a pretty good idea but wanted her to confirm my suspicions.

"If you don't," I'd threatened, "I'll tell everyone on the bus about that time you laughed so hard at the movies that you farted and cleared out all the seats around you."

Her cheeks deepened with red slashes. "Teresa, you wouldn't!"

I nodded. Sometimes you had to fight dirty to save someone from becoming a fool.

She'd dragged me out of earshot from our fellow bowlers and whispered, "Keith gave me a prize for winning. And let me tell you, girlfriend, it wasn't a bar of soap this time." She placed the back of her hand to her forehead as if she was going to swoon like Scarlett O'Hara. "I'll kill you if you tell the others!"

"Tell them what? What did you do with Keith?"

"Take one guess." Her face turned bright red.

I heaved a heavy sigh. "I'm not going to tell the girls, but I think you made a huge mistake fooling around with Keith. He's a playboy out for a good time. You're never going to see him again after this trip."

Her smile vanished. "So what?" she shot back. "I haven't had a good time in ages. Sometimes you have to take it where you can get it."

"Not at the risk of losing your dignity," I retorted.

"Why don't you mind your business and I'll mind mine, okay, Teresa?" With that she'd stalked away in a huff.

Apparently, her good time didn't last longer than

those fifteen minutes. This morning, Crystal wouldn't look at Keith as he imparted his morning speech. I glanced at Jackie and Annette. Seemed to be déjà vu all over again. Crystal's head was bowed to her lap, and from the way the early morning sunlight slanted upon her face, I could tell her cheeks were damp and her eyes were misted over. It was obvious she'd been crying and was still holding in tears.

That damned Keith! What had he said or done to upset her, besides get her hopes up for a fling? I balled my fists and felt my temperature rise as he crooned into his stupid microphone as if he hadn't a care in the world.

My friends and I had started this trip excited and happy. But in five days, most of them had developed symptoms of sadness, depression, anxiety, or guilt. In Donna's case, she was giddy, which was strange and didn't add up. Still, the common denominator between them all was Keith. He'd done something to each and every one of them to cause them to feel less than the terrific women they were. I just knew it! Whatever it was, he wasn't going to get away with it.

Glancing at him through squinty eyes, the seeds of a plan for exacting some kind of revenge began to form in my mind.

"Today is the twentieth wedding anniversary of one of our couples," he announced, shifting my thoughts. "Happy anniversary to Mike and Anna! Tonight, a bottle of wine will be on me at dinner."

"Thank you, Keith," Mike called from the back of the bus.

As we all clapped and whistled, Mike and Anna accepted congratulations all around.

"Twenty years," Jackie groaned, crossing her arms in a defensive stance. "That's a frickin' lifetime." She was my seatmate today and her usual jovial self.

"Marriage is meant to last a lifetime," I reminded her.

She rolled her eyes, as she did often. "How can anyone stand it? Sleeping with the same man every night for the rest of your life. Boring."

"Some women actually love the men they marry and don't mind sleeping with them. Then there are those of us who don't sleep with our husbands at all and prefer boy toys on the side instead." My elbow prodded her in the rib. When I saw hurt flash in her eyes, I quickly apologized. "Sorry, Jackie. I was just teasing. I know Milton's old and sick, and you didn't marry him for his body."

"I'm over the hill, too," she said, so low I could barely hear.

"What are you talking about? Fifty is the new forty, remember?"

She shook her head vehemently. "Fifty is a half a century, Teresa. *A half a century*! That's ancient in dog years. I'm an idiot to think a younger man like…Chris would want me."

For the first time in a long time, the wall Jackie had built around herself years ago began to crumble in front of my eyes. I squeezed her hand. "Is this really about Chris or someone else? Has someone told you you're old?" I couldn't bear to utter Keith's name out loud and possibly hear Jackie's confession. I didn't think I could stand a second revelation about what another one of my friends had done with him. My stomach tightened waiting for her response.

Her gaze jerked toward me, and her teeth gritted as she spoke quietly. "Chris has sex with me because he's young and horny and he'll sleep with anyone who has boobs. He doesn't care about my emotions or my wellbeing. When we get home, I'm telling him it's over. All men are pigs."

"Most, maybe, but not all. Your current husband is not a pig."

She looked at me like I was stupid. "You're right. Milton's not an animal. He's a vegetable in pajamas."

"I thought all his money was supposed to make you happy. You sure don't seem happy lately," I said.

She shrugged her shoulders and then turned the tables on me. "Are you going to marry Phil?"

I laughed so loud I mumbled an apology to those around me before clapping my hand over my mouth. "You're really good at changing the subject."

"Are you?" she pressed.

"I don't even know how long this thing with him will last. Besides, I'm too set in my ways to marry. The matrimony train has passed me by."

"Does Phil know that?" Her curious gaze delved into me.

"Sure, he does. He's been married before. We're both fine with the way it is right now."

"I don't believe you," Jackie challenged.

My temper sparked because she'd hit a nerve. I'd have to be blind not to see the way Phil gazed at me with those puppy dog eyes of his. I had a feeling he did want to marry again, and I was the woman he wanted to hitch his wagon to. The idea scared the crap out of me, so instead of being honest with Jackie, I lashed out, quietly. "I don't care what you believe," I whispered. "Fix your own life before you start psychoanalyzing mine."

She turned her head and stared out the window. And just like that, we weren't speaking to each other.

~ * ~

"Little Bighorn was called the Battle of the Greasy Grass by the Crows," a park ranger in a green uniform told our group.

Shivering in our lightweight jackets and sweatshirts, because it was really cold out, we all stood on Last Stand Hill overlooking the great plains and the battlefield where markers poked up through the waving grass showing where the Seventh Calvary fell, including the spot where Custer supposedly died. An obelisk was engraved with each soldier's name. I was surprised to see a separate marker memorializing the Seventh Calvary horses that had been killed during Custer's Last Stand. According to the park ranger, many of the horses had been buried there.

We also saw a contemporary Indian Memorial that people had tied ribbons and bandanas onto. Then we strolled through the Bighorn National Monument museum before getting back on the bus and starting the long drive to Deadwood, South Dakota.

"That was interesting," Kim said, settling next to me since Jackie was still peeved. "I feel sorry for the Native Americans. They only wanted to be left alone on their land. Our people never have done right by their people, even to this day." After a few moments of silent reflection, she said, "Do you remember the guy that came in with the carnival the summer before we turned sixteen? The one who liked me?"

"The Mexican?" I conjured a fuzzy recollection of a tall brown boy with black hair to his shoulders.

"He wasn't a Mexican. Adam was part Indian, and he wanted to marry me."

"Marry you?" I chuckled. "You were fifteen."

"He said we could have a good life on the road."

"Doing what? Setting up the Ferris wheel, eating cotton candy for supper, and sleeping in the back of a pickup truck? How romantic." That last comment was said sarcastically, of course.

She didn't laugh. "Make fun if you want, but Adam was the first boy to tell me he loved me. I really missed him when the carnival pulled out that summer. When he left, he said he'd be back the following summer and he hoped I'd be ready to run away with him. But he wasn't with the troop the next summer. I never saw or heard from him again. That was the first time my heart was broken."

"You didn't…you know…?"

"Sleep with him?" Kim shook her head. "No, but not for his lack of trying. I was too afraid of getting pregnant. That would have killed my folks to have two daughters knocked up and unwed."

Kim's sister had been the first girl in Harley's Grove to be allowed to continue high school while being pregnant—a big deal for the time period. Her determination to finish school despite waddling around like a beach ball and being ridiculed behind her back had caused Kim's family a great deal of humiliation. Suddenly, I felt a newfound respect for Kim. It took maturity for a fifteen-year-old to consider her parents' feelings above her own. I was proud she hadn't slept with the carnie.

I began to think back to the times she'd put others' needs and desires before her own. There were many examples I remembered, which was commendable, but I couldn't help but ponder whether she'd been doing the same thing for the past ten years by living with Eddie without a wedding and marriage certificate.

"How come you never told me all this about Adam before?" I asked.

"I don't know. I thought I had, or that you knew. The six of us didn't have many secrets between us back then, did we?"

Maybe not then, but I was certain Kim was keeping a secret from us now.

CHAPTER SIXTEEN
Don't Worry, Be Happy

"What kind of a tour company gives a tour of Deadwood without stopping at the cemetery where Wild Bill Hickok and Calamity Jane are buried?" That was Donna grumbling, after we'd stepped down from the trolley that showed us some of the hot spots around the historic South Dakota town.

"The kind of a tour company that Kevin Costner owns, I guess," replied Barb. "Why do you think we were taken to the Midnight Star Casino? Because he owns the bar and restaurant, that's why. They just wanted us to spend money on lunch and drinks. More money in his already deep pockets."

"I did enjoy seeing the costumes he's worn from his movies displayed in the glass cases that way," Winnie said.

"I would have preferred being immersed in the history of the area," Donna said. "This was Indian and gold prospecting country. That tour focused on the casinos and gift shops."

"Nobody let Crystal into a casino," Kim said, teasing our friend. "Remember what happened in Vegas?"

"What happened?" Barb asked.

"It wasn't pretty, that's all I'm saying."

"You want history?" I said to Donna, pointing to Saloon Number 10. "This is where Bill Hickok was shot while playing poker. You want to go in?"

"Of course!" Donna pushed through the door, not waiting for the rest of us.

"You guys see all the history you want," Jackie said. "I'm going shopping. There looks to be some cute boutiques on this street."

"I'll come with you," Kim said. "I haven't gotten anything to take home to Eddie yet."

"I want some earrings made from Black Hills gold," Crystal said.

"What about you, Annette?" I asked. Her anxiety level had increased since her birthday. I'd noticed her digging into her purse more often for one pill or another, but I hadn't had a chance to get her alone to talk since Yellowstone. "Want to go in and see where Wild Bill met his demise?"

She shrugged apathetically. "Sure. Why not?"

Our three friends waved goodbye and strolled down the sidewalk to check out the gift shops.

"I'm pooped," said Winnie, limping toward a bench shaded by the side of a building. "Think I'll rest here a while." She removed a tissue from her purse and wiped perspiration from her face. "It's gotten warm out."

Barb joined her on the bench and motioned us on. "I'll sit with Winnie and rest my feet. You girls have fun. We'll see you later on the bus."

Before we entered the saloon, I pulled Annette aside. "Are you okay? Is there anything you want to talk about? Ever since your birthday, you've been acting weird. I'm your friend. You can confide in me."

The muscle in her jaw twitched. "Can't you get it through your thick head, Teresa? I don't want to talk. I just want to forget about it."

"About what?" I prodded, ignoring the bite in her voice. When my question got no reply, I took the more direct approach I was known for. "Does your change in behavior have something to do with Keith?"

The truth showed itself when her mouth twisted into a grimace. "Just leave it alone, will you?"

"No, I won't. If he hurt you or made you do something you didn't want to do, we need to tell somebody. The tour company, or the police." I grasped at straws trying to get her to open up, because I knew guilt and shame when I saw it. As she stood there with her mouth clamped tight, all I could think about was how I'd like to castrate that devil for whatever he'd done.

Annette grabbed my arm, and her long nails felt like claws when they dug into my skin. "Like an idiot, I got drunk and behaved badly. I'm to blame. Now drop it, Teresa." Her breath hitched, and she shoved me through the door of the saloon.

I knew her dysfunctional home life may have started to affect her decision making, but she wasn't to blame for whatever had happened between her and Keith. With every new revelation that slipped out of the mouths of my friends, I realized Keith was a predator of the worst kind. My heart beat out an angry staccato.

It didn't take long to walk through Saloon Number 10 and view the slot machines, gaming tables, and the spot where Hickok apparently met his maker with the assistance of Crooked Nose Jack McCall. When we exited, two actors dressed like gamblers from the 1800s stood on the curb and offered to pose with us for photos. Annette, Donna and I handed our cameras to a stranger passing by and jostled for spots between the longhaired men. The one I stood next to put his arm around my waist and squeezed my love handle.

"Don't smile," the actor with a bushy mustache said. He kind of reminded me of Phil. "Look mean. Nobody smiled in Deadwood in the 1800's."

We all pursed our lips as the man snapped a picture with each of our cameras. "Thank you!" we said in unison, when he returned out cameras. "Goodbye," we called to the actors as they sauntered toward the next group of vacationers.

I glanced at my watch. "We have two hours to kill before we have to be back on the bus. What do you ladies want to do first?" I asked Donna and Annette. "Eat, gamble, or shop?" Before they could answer, my cell phone rang. It was Crystal asking if we wanted to meet them for lunch.

"Jackie has some news," she said.

"Good or bad?" I feared she'd gotten word that Milton had died.

"She's not thrilled," Crystal said, "but Kim and I are excited."

Could that response have been any more cryptic? I had no idea what was going on. When we reached the restaurant and joined them at a table, Jackie looked pissed, like someone had told her the mansion, the cars, and all of Milton's money had gone up in flames.

"What's up?" Donna asked.

"Madison's engaged," Jackie said. "She called me on my cell about thirty minutes ago."

Madison was Jackie's daughter from her second husband. She was a recent college graduate and had been dating a boy for two years that she'd met at school. They were both good kids, as far as I knew. Madison spent as little time as possible with Jackie, and when she did, they butted heads. But I figured that was typical of a girl her age. It was a good sign that she'd called her mother to give her the news rather than let her find out through the grapevine.

"Congratulations!" I said.

"That's not all," Crystal said, looking like the cat that slurped up all the cream. "Looks like there'll be a wedding at the mansion before the leaves turn colors."

"A fall wedding? Why so soon?" Annette's eyebrow arched.

Jackie slapped her hand on the table. "Stupid girl is pregnant. She's ruined her life now for sure. I should know. I've been there, done that, as we all know."

"Come on," Kim said, calmly. "Madison isn't stupid. In fact, I think she's a very intelligent young woman who knows her own mind, and her heart. Her fella loves her, you've said so yourself. They're going to be fine. Both of them are college graduates. They'll make a great home for their baby, your grandchild. Think of it, Jackie. A baby! I'm so happy for them, and for you!"

My gaze landed on Kim and then shifted to Crystal. Unlike me, the two of them had wanted children. Conflicting emotions of joy and regret crossed their faces.

Jackie placed her head in her hands and whined, "I'm not old enough to be a grandma."

The five of us gazed at each other. Whether we'd admitted it out loud or not, each of us worried about what getting older meant in the scheme of life, love, and sex. This vacation was supposed to have helped us accept the inevitable with grace. I wasn't sure any of us had evolved to that point yet. In fact, it seemed the opposite had taken place. The perfect storm of insecurity coinciding with meeting Keith had spiraled into a tornado, apparently leading to choices that made my friends feel worse about themselves, not better. I felt to blame since coming on this trip had been my idea.

"Yes, you are old enough," I said quietly, but firmly. My hand slipped over Jackie's. "And I pray, when you get over the shock, you'll wear the title of grandma like a badge of honor. A baby is something to celebrate, not to regret." My gaze moved around the table. "I've been thinking. It would do us all good to make the Serenity Prayer our mantra. Do you know it?" I didn't wait for anyone to answer before reciting it. "Oh, God, grant me the serenity to accept the things I cannot change, the courage to change the things I can, and the wisdom to know the difference." I paused for effect. "The moral is, we should all stop fretting about the things that are beyond our control, like growing older, and be content. We're only turning fifty, for God's sake. We're not stepping into the grave!"

After a few moments in which Jackie blew her nose and dabbed at her eyes, the rest of my friends nodded at each other. Jackie straightened up in her chair. "How'd you get to be so damned smart, anyway, Teresa?"

"Must be all that brain food I eat," I joked. They all knew I loved my junk food.

~ * ~

Later, Wayne drove us toward Rapid City, our stop for the night. It had been a long and tiring day. After watching a short video about Mount Rushmore, nearly everyone on the bus was napping. The chorus of snores and soft whistles didn't bother me. My own eyes were closed, and I was about to drift into a sweet dreamland when I sensed a presence nearby. Then I smelled Keith's cologne and heard him address Kim in a low murmur. She was sitting in front of me, also in the aisle seat. I pretended to be asleep while perking my ears.

"I saw you in the gift shop today," he whispered. "When you were looking at the jewelry."

"So?" she whispered back.

"I don't think you understand, Kim. I *saw* you," he repeated.

What was he up to now? I wanted so badly to open my eyes and tell him to crawl back into his hole and leave my friends alone.

"It's none of your business," she said quietly. "I've asked you to leave me alone."

This was the second time I'd overheard a similar conversation between them.

"It'll be police business if I decide to give them a call." He paused for effect, and I could almost hear Kim's breath leave her body. "We need to talk," he said. "Tonight."

I opened my eyes just a crack so he wouldn't notice and saw him stuff a slip of paper into her hand before returning to his seat behind Wayne.

Once, when we were basking in the afterglow of an enthusiastic romp, Phil had asked me, if I could have any super power, what would it be? He brought up silly stuff like that at the most inappropriate times, but that was part of his charm.

Right then, as I speculated as to what Keith's note to Kim said, I sure wished I had the ability to see through objects. Unless I didn't let Kim out of my sight for the rest of the night, there was no way I'd learn what was going on with those two. I might have been regarded as a superhero by my friends, but I sure didn't see how I was going to pull that one off.

CHAPTER SEVENTEEN
The Straw That Broke The Camel's Back

When I woke up the next morning, a deep chill enveloped my body like I'd been sleeping in a snowdrift. It was the last day of our tour before flying home tomorrow, and a sixth sense told me the day wouldn't end well.

"I can't believe our vacation is almost over," Donna said, while applying makeup in the bathroom mirror.

"Have you had a good time?" Trying to shake off the icy thread winding its way up my spine, I held two shirts up and debated which to wear for our outing to the Crazy Horse Memorial and Mount Rushmore.

Donna zipped up her makeup bag and ran a brush through her hair. "Yes, I have," she said, answering my question with a smile. "It's been wonderful. I'm so glad you suggested it and that I spent the money to come. It's been worth every penny. Thank you."

Making my wardrobe decision, I slipped the pink tee shirt over my head and stepped into the bathroom to collect my toiletries. Now seemed like the perfect time to bring up the conversation we'd had a few days ago about her finances. "Remember when you told me

Keith was helping you sort out your financial issues and you said you'd tell me more details at the end of the week?"

She nodded and began brushing her teeth.

I tossed our damp towels into a pile on the floor and wiped the counter with a tissue while waiting for her to finish with her teeth. When she did, I said, "Well, it's the end of the week."

Donna walked into the bedroom and calmly, silently re-packed her suitcase. She'd always had a knack for ignoring a person if she didn't want to talk. Even if she didn't want to discuss this subject, there wasn't much she could do to get away from me. I could be a pit bull when I wanted to be, and I was prepared to block the exit door with my body if she tried to escape before answering my question.

Finally, she snapped her suitcase shut and sat on the bed. She laid her hands in her lap and fiddled with her wedding band. I sat next to her, breathing deeply and feeling I was about to hear another disclosure that would make me want to ring someone's neck.

"The thing is," she began, "Keith told me about this job that will give me the opportunity to earn extra income. He has a couple of women friends who are involved, and he assured me the pay is almost too good to be true. The best part is there's no experience necessary. I just have to dress nice, be friendly to the client, and behave in a certain way."

My temper sparked. "Donna! Is Keith a pimp? Tell me you're not desperate enough to turn tricks!"

Her eyes enlarged. "What?" When her shock ebbed a moment later, she laughed and slapped my arm, a little harder than I thought was necessary. "You dummy. I'm not going to start hooking. Have you ever heard of mystery shopping?"

Mystery shopping? That was pretty much the last thing I expected to hear. Mental fatigue hummed along my nerves. "I think so. Maybe. I'm not sure."

She filled me in. "It's a perfectly legitimate tool used by market research companies or companies themselves to measure a store's quality of service, compliance with regulation, or to gather specific information about products and services. As a mystery shopper, I'll purchase a product, ask questions, register complaints, and behave a certain way, and then provide feedback on my experience. Then they send me a big check for my trouble. Easy peasy."

"When something sounds too good to be true, it usually is," I said. An uneasy feeling slid over my collarbone and settled between my shoulder blades. "What's the catch?"

"There's no catch."

My eyes narrowed. "Exactly how is Keith involved?"

She cleared her throat. "He's the middle man. A restaurant or grocery store will hire him to hire the mystery shopper. He doesn't earn enough being a tour director to live comfortably, so he does this on the side. He takes a cut from each job."

Something was rotten in the state of Denmark, or in South Dakota, as was more the case. "You're going to do this in Harley's Grove?" It didn't make sense. There weren't but a handful of downtown businesses anymore. None of them could afford that kind of service. "How does Keith find these clients in small towns like ours?"

"Larger businesses in the bigger cities are the clients," she clarified. "I'll probably have to drive to Champaign or Bloomington. We haven't worked out the details yet. But I'll get paid to shop and dine, and all that was required was an up-front fee to join."

A red flag flew up in front of my eyes. "What kind of fee?" I barked. "And to whom did you pay this fee?"

The lines around her mouth tightened. "You don't have to bite my head off, Teresa. I wrote Keith a check. He told me there was only one position left in the organization. If I didn't grab it now, another position might not open up for months. It seemed like such a good opportunity."

Not believing what I was hearing, I repeated my previous question. "How much money did you give Keith?" When she told me the amount, it took all my willpower not to throttle her. "How could you hand over your hard-earned money to a scam artist? Because that's what Keith is, pure and simple."

"He's not!"

My gaze searched her innocent face. "Don't you know anything about the Federal Trade Commission?"

"No. Why should I?"

"If you did, you wouldn't have been such a gullible horse's ass." My mouth ran like a stampede of horses, but there was no stopping it now.

Donna's eyebrow lifted in defiance. "How dare you call me an ass, Teresa! What's the FTC got to do with mystery shopping?"

"The FTC regulations state that under no circumstances should anyone be forced to pay a fee in order to obtain a job in the United States, and that would include this ridiculous mystery shopping job." I knew about the FTC because of an employee at the trucking company that had been scammed by a previous employer. My temperature rose like a kettle set to boil. "Keith has scammed you."

Slowly, her face grew ashen. "He wouldn't, I'm telling you."

"Why are you defending him? Because he has a pretty face and a body like Adonis, and you've been lonely since Chad died, and you enjoyed the attention? You don't know him from Adam, Donna. Keith would, and he did scam you! You've got to tell him you made a mistake and you want your money back. Or at least stop payment on the check."

Her lips quivered, and she looked like she was going to cry. "It's too late. He's already cashed my check."

"How do you know?"

"He…he told me last night," she stammered. "He said everything's set. I gave him my email address, and he promised to contact me soon after I get home to give me my first assignment. I trusted him."

"A lot of women trusted Ted Bundy, too." Instead of shrieking, I smoothed my face into a blank mask. "Keith has balls of steel to take advantage of a nearly penniless widow."

Donna's eyes squeezed together, and she pounded her fist on the mattress. "You're right, Teresa. I *am* a jackass. I feel so foolish."

I tried to put myself in her shoes and took a deep breath to calm down. "Don't be. You weren't the first to be swept off your feet by Keith and you won't be the last, unless he's stopped. He knew the right things to say and do to win you over. It's not your fault."

"Did he win you over?" she asked hesitantly.

"No, but I've been told I give off a vibe."

Donna didn't seem inclined to ask what I meant by that comment. "I'll probably never get my money back," she said, staring blankly into space. Then the floodgates suddenly opened and tears splashed down her cheeks. "What am I going to do?" she sobbed. "I gave him everything I have left."

We stared at each other for several long moments. Then I patted her hand. "Try not to worry. I'll figure something out."

~ * ~

After breakfast, Wayne drove us into the Black Hills to our first stop, the Crazy Horse Memorial. Keith stood in the front of the bus wearing his usual khaki shorts and tee shirt talking into his microphone.

"South Dakota is famous for Mount Rushmore, but it's also making room for a second colossal mountain carving that, when finished someday, will dwarf the four presidents. The sculpture in progress is of the Lakota warrior, Chief Crazy Horse, astride a stallion with his arm and pointed hand stretched out over the horse's mane. The monument, taller than the Washington Monument and well over two football fields wide, has been sixty-four years in the making. Sculptor Korczak Ziolkowski began the project in 1948. His wife and seven of their children took up the project after her husband's death in 1982. By the late 1990s, the face of Crazy Horse had emerged from the mountain carving. The last decade has been spent roughing out the horse's head, which is twenty-two stories high."

"That's a huge undertaking," Crystal whispered into my ear. "I doubt Crazy Horse will ever be finished. The sculptor's family will all be dead someday, and that'll be the end of it." When she noticed my gaze riveted to Keith, she elbowed me in the rib. "Did you hear me, Teresa?"

My gaze jerked toward her. "Sure. You were talking about dead people."

"No, not exactly."

I lowered my voice. "Crystal, have you ever hated someone so much you wanted to kill them?"

There was no hesitation on her part. "Yes. My ex-husband."

"I guessed that much. Anyone else?" When my gaze flicked back to Keith, her eyes followed and I felt her tense beside me.

"There have been people who've caused me so much pain that I've wished them dead at the moment," she confessed, "but everyone thinks stuff like that at one time or another. It's just a reaction when you've been hurt or you're really angry. No one really means it." We both stared at Keith for what seemed like an eternity before Crystal quietly added, "Everyone has some kind of darkness inside them. What separates us from animals is not acting on that darkness."

The depth of her statement surprised me. "I might be able to commit murder, if given the right provocation," I blurted.

Her mouth gaped. She whispered, "Are you insane? What would be the right kind of provocation?"

The memory of something that happened to me a

long time ago emerged like a creature rising up from the dark lagoon. My heart thundered beneath my tee shirt. I stuck my hands under my thighs to keep Crystal from seeing them shake.

"We're all responsible for our actions," I finally said. "People who do wrong by others should get what they deserve."

CHAPTER EIGHTEEN
The Truth Is Revealed

We had just unloaded at Mount Rushmore when Mike made an announcement to the group. "I just got a call on my cell phone from our son in Atlanta. Anna and I are grandparents of a healthy bouncing baby boy! He weighed in at twenty pounds and seven inches!"

Anna laughed and playfully smacked his arm. "It's the other way around, Mike! By your measurements, he's either a worm or an extremely large pumpkin."

"Whatever," he said, excitedly. "I gave up smoking cigars years ago, so it's chocolate covered cherries for everyone!"

They'd been waiting since yesterday morning to hear that their daughter-in-law had given birth. Mike had bought the candy at a shop in Deadwood in anticipation. As he eagerly passed the chocolates out, Keith explained the remainder of the day's schedule.

"You'll have two hours here at your leisure, and then we'll drive through Bear Country USA, a wildlife park, on our way to the hotel. Tonight, for those who wish to, we'll return to Mount Rushmore for the evening lighting program, which is really spectacular.

If you need to do some last minute shopping, check out the gift shop (he pointed in the general direction), and there's a café where you can grab lunch and a snack bar which serves some really good ice cream for you folks with a sweet tooth. But before you all break off on your own, let's gather for a group photo to commemorate our time together."

All forty of us followed him and Wayne to a spot along a low wall where the backdrop for the photo was a clear view of the four presidents: Washington, Jefferson, Teddy Roosevelt and Lincoln.

After posing for the professional photograph, my five friends and I passed through the patriotic Walkway of Flags and then took our time hiking along the wooden boardwalk path called the Presidential Trail. Every bend offered a different vantage point of the sculptures carved into the granite face of the mountain. The scenery and carvings were far more dramatic and beautiful than I'd imagined they'd be. For that short time when we were laughing and snapping pictures, I forgot all about Keith and my plan for revenge.

"Do you guys remember the Hitchcock movie, *North by Northwest?*" Annette asked. We stood on a wooden platform at a point so close to the mountain that we were looking almost directly into the presidents' faces. "In the movie, when Cary Grant and Eva Marie Saint are dangling from the presidents' faces, it looks like they're miles high up on the mountain, but apparently they weren't."

"I love that movie," Kim said. "Why don't they make men like Cary Grant anymore? He was so handsome and sophisticated, and debonair."

"He was married five times," Donna said. "Why would you want a man who can't commit?" As soon as the words left her mouth, she realized what she'd said, but it was too late to reel them back in. "Sorry, Kim. I wasn't thinking."

"Forget it. We all know Eddie is never going to marry me."

That was the first time I'd heard her say it out loud.

"Poor Kim," Crystal said, flinging an arm around her shoulders. Just be thankful you have a man to go home to, unlike me. And who cares if you haven't walked down the aisle? At least you're not Jackie. One more wedding and she'll be tied with 'ol Cary Grant. By the way, Jackie, have you chosen your next husband yet? There are a couple of fellas on this tour who would be happy to accommodate." Crystal chuckled, but the rest of us didn't.

Jackie's eyes grew as hard as bullets. "No more husbands for me. Milton is the last. He's the only man I've ever known who isn't a pig." She stepped off the trail and dropped onto a bench under a tree. Glad for shade, we joined her. "I hope Milt's still alive when we get home," she said, softly. "I want to tell him how much I've appreciated him and all he's done for me. He probably won't understand, but it'll make me feel better to say it."

Surprised at her sentimentality, I covered her hand with mine. "That's a great idea, Jackie. Milton *has* been good to you. Because of him, you'll never want for anything material for the rest of your life."

We all sat together, listening to birdsong, feeling the soft breeze blow through our hair, and watching the tourists. Unfortunately, the talk of men got me to thinking about Keith again, and my mood sank. Apparently, I wasn't the only one with the same reaction.

"I slept with Keith," Annette blurted. Five pair of eyes regarded her with shock and then curiosity. Despite the warm weather, her body began to shake like she was standing naked in a river on a February morning. "This secret has been killing me. I need to tell you what happened. Let me get it out before I change my mind," she said, not returning our gazes. Her voice trembled as she explained.

"It happened the night of my birthday in Jackson. As you all know, I drank too much and Keith volunteered to walk me back to the Antler Inn. Instead of going straight to my room, however, we went to his room for a nightcap. He kissed me and told me I was beautiful, and, well, one thing led to another. You can imagine the rest. There's no need to fill you in on the gory details. Obviously, I wasn't thinking straight, and I was so angry with Bruce for not even calling to wish me a happy birthday. I suppose that's why I let it happen. Bruce and I have been increasingly growing apart, and Dustin moving home has made things even more stressful. To be honest, I'm not sure my husband and I love each other anymore. But that's no excuse for sleeping with another man," she said quickly.

Several heartbeats passed in silence. Then she said, "I felt like a slut when it was over. I've been so ashamed ever since. But you want to know the worst of it?" Probably no one did, but she told us anyway. "I got sick and threw up. Keith got so mad, he literally chucked my clothes at me and told me to get out of his room. Then he shoved me outside half dressed."

Stunned, Kim's hand flew to her mouth.

"Oh, honey. I'm so sorry," Donna said, touching Annette's arm.

Crystal shook her head. "What a disgusting creep. He took advantage of you knowing you were drunk and a married woman. He had no right." She paused before delivering her own bombshell. "Just like he had no right to do what he did to me."

"What are you talking about?" Jackie asked. The rest of us shifted our focus to Crystal.

Evidently, she hadn't told anyone but me that Keith had given her a "prize" for winning at bowling. But what *hadn't* she told me? "What really happened that night at the bowling alley?" I asked her.

She nibbled her lip. "He pulled me into the ladies bathroom and locked the door. I thought that was pretty exciting, just like in the movies. Then he pressed me against the wall and we kissed and his hands roamed all over my body. I felt like I'd fallen into a dream. It's been so long since a man has touched me, and Keith is so…so handsome. I couldn't believe he was attracted to me." She drew in a deep breath.

"Turns out he wasn't attracted to me at all. It was all about a stupid bet he'd made with Wayne. I overheard them talking early the next morning before breakfast when they thought no one was around. Keith told Wayne I was the first farm animal he'd ever had sex with. They both laughed, and I was so humiliated I could have died. I've felt sick to my stomach ever since."

"Did you have sex with him in the bathroom?" Kim asked.

Crystal shook her head emphatically. "No. We just made out like a couple of horny teenagers and then I put the brakes on. I was afraid of getting caught. He lied to Wayne about having sex with me. I'm disgusted and angry about that, but the part that causes me the most pain is…"

"We know," I said. "You don't have to repeat it." Sighing, I looked at Donna, hoping she'd make her own confession so as to show Crystal and Annette they weren't the only ones Keith had hurt.

"Keith took advantage of me, too," she said, meeting my gaze. After explaining her situation about him scamming her out of her savings, I looked at Kim.

"What's he holding over your head?" I asked.

At first she denied anything. "Keith didn't do anything to me."

"We're your friends," I reminded her. "We're not going to judge you. We want to help if you're in trouble. You can trust us."

"I don't have any idea what you're insinuating," she said stubbornly.

I didn't have time for games. "Kim, I overheard Keith question you twice about your shopping habits, and the last time he threatened to call the police. You acted strangely in the gift shop in Utah, and I haven't been able to stop thinking about that box in your closet back home. What did Keith threaten to expose?"

It took some time, but she finally admitted she'd been shoplifting for close to a year. "I don't know why I do it," she said. "It's not like I need any of the things I take. It's a thrill, I guess. I feel powerful when I steal something, even if it's a ridiculous ink pen. The more I get away with it, the more risks I take." She wrung her hands in her lap. "Keith saw me take something and threatened to call the police and turn me in if I didn't…"

"Didn't what?" I was going to toss my cookies if I heard he'd forced her to sleep with him.

"He wanted money in return for his silence, so I gave him all I had to spare. But that wasn't enough. He made me withdraw more from my account at an ATM. I'm still afraid he won't keep his end of the bargain and I'll be arrested. Every time I hear a siren, I think he's called the cops. I'm a stressed-out basket case."

I had a pretty good idea as to why Kim shoplifted. It didn't take a psychoanalyst to understand that this was clearly a psychological issue for her. It had nothing to do with greed or poverty. Shoplifting was about struggling with her own personal conflicts and needs. "Kim," I said, "I think I speak for all of us when I say we love you and we want to help you. The first step is for you to recognize you have a problem and then get counseling for it. You can't continue this behavior or you *will* end up in jail. This is serious."

My friends nodded their agreement.

"I know," she said. "In the beginning, shoplifting made me feel in control, but everything has gone haywire and I feel worse than ever. I'm turning fifty, and I have no husband and no children. Eddie's a bum who doesn't love or respect me enough to marry me. I've wasted my life."

"It's never too late for change. Are you willing to start counseling when we get home?" I asked.

"You have no choice," Jackie chimed in, grabbing Kim's hand. "I will personally call and make the first appointment and drive you to the shrink myself. We can't lose you, Kim, to depression or jail, or whatever. You're too important to us."

"To all of us," Annette reiterated.

"Thank you," she replied, squeezing back tears. "I'll go for counseling. I'm tired of living a double life. I want to be free and happy, like when we were kids."

"Wouldn't that be nice?" Jackie said. "Life was great before men entered the picture." She slipped a cigarette from the pack in her purse and lit it up. After blowing some smoke rings into the air, she said, "Are you guys ready to hear my sob story involving our infamous tour director?"

CHAPTER NINETEEN
Decisions, Decisions…

Jackie had invited Keith to her room for a drink on the night of the rodeo in Utah. She'd flirted with him all day, and yes, she confessed to planning on having sex with him while we were all gone. But when he'd gotten a little rough and verbally abusive during foreplay, she'd changed her mind quickly. When asked, he wouldn't leave the room.

"I thought he was going to rape me. He was strong and determined. Luckily, I'd placed my purse on the bedside table and was able to grab my Mace from the inside pocket. Do you remember he wore sunglasses the next morning? I sprayed him directly in his eyes."

I *had* recalled. We all snickered and were thankful Jackie had been prepared and knew how to defend herself.

"Way to go," Crystal said.

"As he stumbled out the door half blind," Jackie continued, "he had some pretty nasty things to say about my being a worn out hag. He said he has pity sex with a lot of old women on his tours. I would have been no different. Direct quote."

Although Jackie had always been a tough chick, and she was still an attractive woman, it was easy to see his words had cut to the quick. Rage flared, and I coughed to clear the emotion lodged in my throat.

"We should contact someone high up at the bus company," Donna said, balling her fists. "At the very least, Keith needs to be fired and arrested for attempted rape and held accountable for the money he's stolen from me and Kim. We can't let him get away with humiliating and threatening all of us. There are six of us. If we stick together, they'll believe us over him."

"I went to his room willingly," Annette reminded us.

"And there's no law against calling someone names," Crystal said, sadly.

"But the rest of it," Donna pleaded. "We can't let him get away with what he's done to us! There's no doubt he's treated other women this way in the past and he will in the future unless we—"

"Stop him," I interjected. "And we will, Donna. I promise you. Keith Creswell will never hurt another woman again." My insides were raked raw, and I felt my heart pounding wildly.

"What do you have in mind?" Jackie asked.

The word slipped from my mouth as smooth as honey. "Murder."

A chorus of gasps accompanied my friends' wide eyes. "My God! Are you crazy, Teresa?" Kim exclaimed. "Even if you hate someone's guts, you can't murder him."

"Why not?" My mouth formed the words, and the voice was mine, but it felt like another entity had taken over my body—someone with a black heart.

"What did Keith do to you?" Annette inquired.

I was far more incensed than I'd let myself believe. "Nothing. But he's degraded all of you. He's probably hurt dozens more women, emotionally and physically. I've never understood why men like him get away with the things they do. They ruin people's lives and never pay for it. If I thought there was another way to stop him, it would be different. But I don't think he can stop his manipulating. When I see how his actions have affected you, I'm so furious I could spit nails." My hands clenched and unclenched at my sides. "I've come up with a plan."

"A plan?" Jackie's jaw dropped. "We just told each other what he's done. How could you have devised a plan already?"

"I'm more observant than you might imagine. I've been thinking about this for a couple of days. Don't worry. I'm not going to involve any of you. I'll handle this alone."

"Handle *what* alone?"

They regarded each other with expressions of doubt and confusion.

"Teresa, I don't think you realize how much we all care about you," Donna said, softly, like I was a bomb that would detonate if she raised her voice. "You're a special person. You've always been strong and smart, and a best friend to each of us. You've helped every single one of us out of jams through the years. But you are not going to commit murder on our behalf. That's just ridiculous, so get it out of your head right now!"

"But—"

"There are no buts about it," Jackie said, firmly.

"Together, we'll think of some way to make him pay, short of criminal activity."

"Killing him is not the answer," Kim agreed. "No one gets away with murder. If you go to prison, who will plan our next vacation?"

I stared at her thinking I'd misheard. Then Kim's mouth twitched into a smile. Crystal chuckled, and within moments, we were all holding our stomachs from laughing hard.

For the past two days, I'd felt like I was walking around in a fog. Keith's behavior and a recalled incident from my past had sent me spinning out of control. But with Kim's last comment meant to lighten the mood, the fog suddenly lifted. *Get a grip*, I told myself. I didn't have the heart of a killer. There was no way I could intentionally set out to murder another human being.

My mouth tilted in an apologetic smile, and I felt my good sense return. "I'm sorry, girls, if I scared you. You're right. No matter what Keith has done, murder is not the answer."

"Thank God you came to your senses," Annette breathed. "Do you promise to forget you had such an idiotic thought?"

I crossed my heart with a finger. "Promise."

They heaved a collective sigh of relief, and Annette glanced at her watch. "None of us expected this conversation to take place today. It's been difficult for all of us, admitting our weaknesses and vulnerabilities, but maybe now that everything is out in the open, we can do better to support each other from now on. Although it's going to be hard, I suggest we try to forget about Keith for the time being and enjoy our final day of vacation."

"We do have a schedule to adhere to," Kim added. "If we want to eat lunch before returning to the bus, we'd better hustle."

After a group hug, we made our way to the café. Although nothing had been settled, not really, the cloud of uncertainty that had briefly driven some of us apart seemed to have lifted.

When it was time to load onto the coach, I purposefully sat in a seat further back next to Winnie and away from my girlfriends. After confessing my notion to murder Keith, there was no way I could look him—or them—in the eyes, because, if the truth were told, I still wanted to kill him.

During the drive through the wildlife preserve, in which he pointed out dozens of beautiful animals, the same darkness that had threatened to swallow me many years ago covered me like a blanket. An icy chill numbed my body. Although I'd promised the girls not to seek revenge on Keith, a feeling hinted that he'd still be dead before the tour ended.

~ * ~

After breakfast the next morning, Wayne drove us through the Black Hills National Forrest where Ponderosa pines, spruce and aspen forests provide a home for a variety of wildlife. From there, we continued on through the National Grassland prairies of South Dakota and Wyoming en route to Colorado's capital city of Denver.

The mood on the bus was sedate. Everyone had grown close and would miss the new friendships we'd developed. That night we'd gather for a farewell dinner and short program at our hotel. The next day, all travelers would depart at various times to the Denver International Airport for our return home.

Throughout the long day's drive, my nerves twitched under my skin. Every time my gaze connected with Keith's, I pictured him hurting my friends, and my body went as rigid as a steel shaft. As he lectured, I visualized several scenarios, all of which ended with him planted six feet underground. No matter how I tried to shake away the images, I couldn't stop thinking of ways to murder him.

Poison in food or drink worked well in many of the murder mysteries I'd read through the years. I could see Keith knocking back a cold beer at the farewell dinner and then clutching his throat and writhing on the floor as the poison flowed through his veins and shut down his internal organs. But where would I get the poison? That kind of crime had to be planned way ahead of time.

Another popular way to commit murder was by stabbing. In that fantasy, the six of us hid our steak knives from dinner in our fanny packs, shoved Keith into a dark hallway, and each took a stab at him, like the people did in Agatha Christie's novel, *Murder on the Orient Express*. But that vision quickly dissolved, because I didn't want my friends involved.

I remembered a famous case some years back and a more recent one where betrayed wives had sliced off their husbands' penises and disposed of them. That form of punishment seemed appropriate. I gave it some consideration before realizing I'd have to put myself in an intimate situation with Keith for that to work. That was something I was unwilling to do.

There were all manners of clever ways in which to do away with someone. The problem was, did Keith really deserve to die? Or had he behaved as a pig-dog because women allowed him to? Why did men think they could take advantage of women? And why did women let them get away with it? I slumped in my seat and closed my eyes knowing it was an age-old question that would probably never be answered.

My macabre musings were disrupted when the memory of that night so long ago skated through my mind. After successfully keeping it tucked in a hidden place for so long, the flashes that had been coming over the past couple of days suddenly burst into a full blown slow-motion picture.

My body broke into a cold sweat, and a soft groan tore from my chest. All my senses heightened. I could smell that same strong cologne. Inside my head, my voice cried out in pain. I heard the horrible grunting and felt the tear of flesh. Squeezing my eyes shut, I tried to mentally erase the horrible image from my mind. Thankfully, Winnie's voice drew me back to the here and now.

"I'm sure going to miss you ladies. You've been a lot of fun to travel with." She patted my hand. "I hope we'll stay in touch. Who knows? Maybe we'll even travel together again someday."

I smiled, doing my best to staunch my shaking hand.

"I'm going to book my next tour as soon as I get home," she said.

"Are you? Where will you be headed next time?" Did I sound normal? I had no idea. Hopefully, Winnie wouldn't notice I was emotionally falling apart.

"Wherever Keith is the tour director," she answered with a wink. "Being around him this week has been like a shot of adrenaline to my heart. I've been depressed since my husband died, and at times I didn't want to go on living myself. I poured my soul out to Keith one night, and he was so kind and compassionate. He convinced me that life is worth living, even if I have to live it alone. His words have done me a world of good."

Incredulous, I stared at her. Was this the same man who had threatened my friends, stolen their money and their dignity, and verbally and physically attacked them? The same man I'd been fantasizing about murdering?

I forced the knot out of my tongue and gave her a weak smile. "I hope you have a great time, wherever you go," I said, sincerely.

Wherever Winnie went, it wouldn't be with Keith. Because as you and I both know, he would never direct a tour again.

CHAPTER TWENTY
End of the Road

Our farewell banquet meal in Denver was worse than terrible. The salad was dry, the rolls were hard, and the chicken entrée was lukewarm. Even Chuck, whom we'd dubbed the human garbage disposal, complained about the lackluster send off. "At least the booze was good," he chuckled.

Once dessert was served, we sat through an hour of our fellow travelers sharing their favorite memories of the trip. Then the five amigas performed a little skit they'd written, complete with poetry, song and dance. They dedicated it to *our wonderful tour director who made this trip so special.*

If I hadn't been concerned about drawing attention to myself, I would have shoved my fingers down my throat and puked.

Finally, Keith took to the podium and mike to say a few words to close out the evening. As usual, his hair was perfect, his clothes accentuated his muscles and fine physique, and his teeth sparkled brighter than radioactive diamonds. But his slurred speech was evidence that he was a little more than tipsy. Having kept my eye on him throughout the evening, I'd noticed he drank a lot of beers.

"First of all," he began, "I'm sure you all noticed Wayne isn't with us tonight. He had to turn the bus around almost the moment we arrived in Denver and head back for Las Vegas, where he'll be starting another tour in two days. He wanted me to wish you all safe travels home, and he hopes you'll join us for another tour in the near future."

Admiring eyes of the many senior ladies beamed as Keith then spoke of his delight in getting to know all of us. "It's been my pleasure to share my love for the magnificent west, along with its history, scenery, and people. As some of you might know, my home base is right here in Denver. This is where I was born and raised. If any of you find your way back to the Mile High City in the future, be sure and look me up. I'll be happy to give you the grand tour of my hometown. Thank you again for traveling with us! Sleep well tonight, and safe journeys tomorrow."

Amidst a round of applause, Keith smiled and waved and then staggered out of the room. With the life of the party gone, everyone else was apparently ready to call it a night. The men and women we'd grown fond of during the past nine days gave out hugs and email addresses while saying their goodbyes. The six of us were some of the last to leave the banquet room.

"Too bad we don't have Keith's home address," Crystal said, as we strolled down the lobby toward the elevators. "We could egg his house."

"What good would that do?" Donna asked with a smirk. "That won't get my money back."

"Mine, either," Kim said.

Crystal shrugged. "I know, but it might make us feel better to do *something*."

"You know what would make us feel better?" I said.

Jackie took one last puff from her cigarette and crushed it out in the ashtray next to the elevators. She pushed the up button. "Going to bed and trying to forget we ever met Keith Creswell?"

"No. What is the one thing we always rely on to lift our spirits when we're down?"

"Alcohol," Annette said. "Me excluded, of course."

For the first time in a while, we all chuckled. "No. What else?"

"Chocolate and cupcakes?" Kim joked.

"I know," Jackie said, cocking an eyebrow. "Line dancing."

Nodding, I led my friends away from the elevators and toward the pool area outside. The pool was closed but the gate was open, and no one was around. It was a warm and balmy evening in Denver. Stars twinkled in the sky, and I suddenly wanted to dance more than anything in the world. It was the best way to free the black thoughts I'd been having.

We lined up in front of the kidney-shaped pool, and I removed my Kindle Fire Tablet from my purse and turned it on. Within moments I was ready to search my music library. "What song do you feel like dancing to, ladies?"

"How about Dolly Parton's *Romeo*?" Donna suggested. "Makes sense in a weird way."

"I couldn't agree more." After browsing my Cloud, I downloaded the song and set the Kindle on a nearby glass-topped table. Dolly's voice poured out of the tablet singing the words, "a cross between a movie star and a hero in a book, Romeo comes struttin' in and everybody looks." The lyrics perfectly described the man who had screwed my friends (in one case, literally). The beat of the music fired not only my blood, but the blood of my friends. We shoved our fingers into the waistbands of our jeans and shuffled to the steps of the Jive Bunny. The song choice couldn't have been more appropriate, considering.

By the time Dolly sang the chorus, we were clapping, twirling, and belting out the song with her. With every step, my feet pounded the concrete deck as I pretended to stomp on cockroaches—one in particular. It felt so good to release all the pent-up emotion that had been trapped in my body for the last few days.

When the song ended, it was as if six mini volcanoes had erupted. We melted into each other's arms and laughed, hugging one another.

Annette's eyes glistened with fresh tears. "I did some really stupid things on this trip, but I can get through anything as long as I have you guys by my side."

The sound of someone clapping stopped us in our tracks. I glanced over my shoulder to see a lone figure standing near the gate under a ray of moonlight. "Nice job, ladies," the man said.

Our circle broke apart, and we turned simultaneously to face Keith.

Blood surged through me like a speeding train. "What are you doing out here?" I asked. "We thought you'd gone home already."

He sauntered toward us holding a beer bottle in his hand, as if he hadn't already had enough. Wobbling, his legs crashed into a deck chair. "Shit, that hurt! Who put that there?" He shoved the chair out of the way with his foot and continued forward like a lion on the prowl. Once he stood in front of us, his lips lifted in a crooked smile. "I've been waiting for a friend to pick me up, but I heard music."

Reeking of alcohol and strong cologne, his lusty gaze moved from woman to woman, roaming over each of us. My stomach rolled and my fists pumped at my sides. The sickening scents wafting from him stirred a stew of unwanted memories.

"Didn't expect to see you gals out here," he said. "What a pleasant surprise. I've missed your past performances and had no idea you could shake your asses like that."

"Shut up, you pig," Jackie gritted. Despite the dim light reflecting off the lamps around the pool, I could see her eyes fire and blaze.

He raised his hands up as if surrendering and smiled. "Sorry to rile you, sweet cheeks. I didn't mean anything by it. Watching y'all writhe around got me horny, that's all."

"Just leave," she said, stone-faced.

Shaking his head, his eyes narrowed into a wolfish glare. "Not yet." He plunked the beer bottle onto the glass table where my Kindle sat and flopped into a chair. "I want to see more, and this time, I'd like a lap dance." He snapped his fingers like he was the King of Siam summoning a servant to bring him grapes. "Any one of you will do. I'll pick out some sexy music while you decide who the lucky chick is."

When he reached for my Kindle, something inside of me snapped. "Put that down," I said, calmly. Too calmly, my friends would tell me later.

Ignoring me, Keith grabbed for the Kindle, but it slid between his fumbling fingers and dropped to the concrete deck. "Oops," he said, throwing his head back and laughing.

Without thinking, just reacting, I lunged and snatched the beer bottle from the table and smashed it against the side of his head. It must have hit in the perfect spot, because he slumped in the chair without so much as a yelp. Blood spilled from a wound in his scalp and dripped from his ear. Without needing to check his pulse or feel for a heartbeat, I knew he was dead. His body was limp, and no breath escaped from between his lips.

Behind me, I heard a chorus of gasps.

"What have you done?" someone cried.

"Oh, my God. Is he dead?" someone else asked.

Ignoring them because I had to work fast, I grabbed hold of Keith's arms, heaved him from the deck chair, and dragged him to the edge of the pool.

"What are you doing?" Donna asked, throwing her arms around my waist.

I shook her off. "I'm setting up the crime scene. Please move. All of you." Lips grave and brows troubled, their faces petrified into expressions of terrified surprise. I quickly collected the shards of glass from the broken bottle that had scattered and tossed them onto the concrete near the body. Then I hauled the table over. Next, the chair Keith had been sitting in. I tipped it over and arranged it beside his body. My idea was to make it look as if he'd strolled out to the pool drunk, tripped over the chair, fallen and hit his head on the concrete, and smashed the bottle as he fell.

"Teresa, stop this," Crystal begged. "We should tell hotel management what happened. It was an accident."

I glared at her. "It wasn't an accident, and we all know it. I would never ask any of you to lie, but I'll be arrested for murder if we tell anyone. Is that what you want?"

"No," she admitted, after a sob caught in her throat.

"What about the rest of you?" I asked, scanning their horrified faces. "Do you want to tell?" They all shook their heads.

"Okay then." When the setup looked right, I yanked off my tee shirt and wiped down the table and chair of my fingerprints. Then I pulled the shirt back over my head and knelt to shift Keith's head so that his blood dripped onto the concrete.

A gaggle of laughter floated out from somewhere near the pool entrance, causing us all to freeze. My heart ricocheted inside my chest like a pinball. As we waited to see if we were going to be discovered, my mind floated back in time. Staring at the man on the ground, it felt justice had finally been served, and a sense of relief washed over me.

When the laughter drifted back into the hotel, Annette whispered, "Let's get out of here before anyone else wanders out."

"One last thing," I said, standing up. I kicked the corpse as hard as I could in the rib with my foot and muttered, "How do you like being on the receiving end of pain, Roger? It's about time you got what you deserved."

Before my friends could stop me, I rolled him into the pool. It felt as if an empty hole had been filled as I watched the body sink. I knew he'd float to the top soon enough and be found tomorrow morning, most likely by the pool crew. When I turned and met the stunned gazes of my friends, their mouths gaped, and each and every one of them was as pale as a ghost.

"Let's go," Jackie said, grabbing my arm. I snatched my Kindle from the ground and she hustled me through the gate with the others following on our heels. "Act natural," she said, as we slowed our steps and walked into the hotel and nonchalantly made our way to the elevators.

With held breath, we waited for what seemed an eternity for the doors to open. Thankfully, no other passengers were inside. We crowded inside, and Kim pushed the button for our floor and the elevator began to rise. No one said a word until we stumbled into Crystal and Annette's room, the one closest to the elevators.

Annette locked the door behind us, and the six of us huddled together on one of the beds. They were all breathing heavily and trembling. The burden I'd carried for so long melted off my shoulders like snow on a hot tin roof. My body overflowed with peace and tranquility.

"Are you all right, Teresa?" Donna touched my arm gingerly.

I felt myself smile. "Yes. Why?"

They all looked at each other as if I'd lost my mind, which in a way, I had. "Because you just killed Keith, and you called him Roger." Her brows knitted together in alarm.

What was she talking about? "No, I didn't," I argued.

"Yes, you did. You said, how do you like being on the receiving end of pain, Roger? What did you mean by that?"

As quickly as it had appeared, sweet euphoria vanished and the impact of what I'd done, and why, hit me. Although we'd shared nearly every life event with each other since we were children, there was something I'd been keeping from my best friends. After thirty-two years, it was time to tell them my darkest secret.

CHAPTER TWENTY-ONE
Teresa's Secret

"Did I really call him Roger?" I felt like an amnesia victim who'd lost both memory and time.

Five heads nodded. "Who is Roger?" Donna asked again.

After clearing my throat, I slipped my hand into hers to bolster my courage and told my story for the first time ever.

"Near the end of the first semester of my freshman year of college, I was invited to an off-campus party. Some girls from my dorm knew the guys who were throwing it. The guys were senior football players, and they lived in a house. I was pretty excited to be invited, as you can imagine. When we got to the house, music blared. There were several kegs of beer set up, and the rooms were thick with marijuana smoke. Everyone was having a good time. As the night progressed, I smoked a joint and drank a few beers. I was high, but not out of it. Just feeling good, you know?"

Five pairs of sympathetic eyes stared at me, urging me to continue. I inhaled a deep breath and went on. "At one point, I had to go to the bathroom. I couldn't find my friends to ask them where the restroom was. I was looking for them when all of a sudden one of the guys who lived in the house snuck up behind me. He'd been introduced to me earlier in the evening as Roger, the quarterback of the football team. Of course I recognized him right off, because he was one of the most popular guys on campus. Built of pure muscle, he stood over six feet with reddish blond hair, blue eyes, and Robert Redford looks. Apparently, he was smart and one of the few athletes who earned good grades. He was also involved in different clubs on campus and even worked with the Boys and Girls Club and did other volunteer work within the local community. I asked him where the restroom was, and he showed me the way. Although he'd been drinking, he seemed less drunk that most of the other people at the party."

My stomach knotted as I recalled what happened next. "I thanked him, but before I could lock the door, Roger pushed his way inside. He slammed the door shut and bolted it. The next thing I knew, I was on my back on the cold tile floor with my jeans being yanked down. I tried to scream, but he mashed his hand over my mouth and nose, nearly suffocating me. I tried to fight back, but he was so much bigger and stronger. As he forced himself into me, the sickening odor of his strong cologne mixed with beer breath made me gag."

I swallowed the bile that rose in my throat at the memory. "When it was over, I cried and told him he wouldn't get away with it. I'd go to the administration and the police. He slapped my face and threatened me. Then he laughed and said he'd tell everyone it was consensual. No one would believe me. He was the golden boy quarterback who could do no wrong. He said he'd tell everyone I was a slutty girl who screwed the star football player and then tried to ruin his good reputation with lies. He also reminded me that I could get suspended from school, and maybe even arrested, if college administration and police found out I'd been smoking pot and drinking underage."

"Did you tell them anyway?" Crystal asked.

"No. I told no one, not even the girls I went to the party with. I didn't want to get kicked out of school or arrested. I couldn't do that to my parents. Anyway, I didn't figure anyone would believe me, just like Roger had said. He was powerful on campus."

My heart contracted in pain as I remembered the guilt and shame I'd felt, even though it hadn't been my fault and I'd done nothing to warrant the attack. "I tried to forget about it, but shortly afterward, some girls in my dorm told me they'd heard I'd slept with Roger and wanted to know if it was true. Obviously, he was telling people we'd had sex. When I saw the smirks on those girls' faces, I knew they didn't envy or admire me. I was a big joke—just a stupid, starry-eyed girl who had become another notch on the quarterback's bedpost. Mortified, I felt used and abused. I'd been raised to stand up for myself, but that man stripped me of my confidence. I didn't have the guts to tell the truth and press charges. Somehow I made it through finals and then decided to leave school for good. I lied to everyone back home about wanting to find myself. What I really did was suffer in silence."

"Oh, Teresa. I'm so sorry," Kim said, hugging me. My other friends echoed the same sentiments. Their arms surrounded me in a blanket of warmth and love.

Their devotion was genuine, but could they forgive me for what I'd done to Keith? No one had the right to take another human being's life. Feeling I owed them a final explanation, I said, "When I discovered the way Keith had been treating all of you, something snapped. All I could think about was what that monster had done to me all those years ago. Both men used their looks and charm to get away with despicable behavior. There'd been no repercussions before. I couldn't let that happen again. But I honestly didn't intend for it to play out the way it did. I hope you believe me."

Tears and understanding glistened in their eyes.

"Why didn't you ever tell us?" Annette asked.

I shook my head. "You've always looked up to me. How could I let you down? Ever since we were kids, I've been the strong one in the group. I couldn't admit that I'd been too scared and weak to do the right thing. I should have gone to the police and pressed charges, even if it meant being kicked out of school or getting put through the wringer at a trial. But I didn't. I don't know how many girls Roger forced himself onto before me, or how many came after. The fact that I did nothing haunts me to this day."

"It's time for you to let it all go," Jackie said. "Roger, Keith, the responsibility you've carried all these years, all of it." Her gaze locked onto mine and she squeezed my hands. "You were angry with Keith for what he did to all of us, but I know you didn't set out to murder him tonight, no matter what you may have said before. We love you and we'll stand behind you. Won't we?" She searched each of my friends' faces with hope in her eyes.

~ * ~

The next morning, Keith was found floating face down in the pool by a hotel staff member. The police were called and everyone in the hotel who had some connection to him was interviewed. The people from our bus tour who hadn't yet left to catch their flights home sat with us in the lobby, unbelieving. Each person, including the six of us, told the same story when questioned. Keith had drunk a lot at the farewell dinner, and no one had seen him after he left the banquet room.

From what we discerned before boarding the shuttle that would take us to the Denver airport, the police would most likely rule Keith's death an unfortunate accident, one in which there was no one but himself to blame.

CHAPTER TWENTY-TWO
One Year Later

Phil squeezed my butt when I sidled next to him holding a tray filled with opened hamburger buns. "Hey," I laughed. "Focus on your job, Casanova. Are those burgers done yet? We have a hungry crowd waiting."

"They're done," he said, slipping one hamburger at a time off the grill until the buns were filled.

"Thank you," I said, giving him a quick kiss. "Do you know you're my favorite chef?"

"You've told me a few times, but I never tire of hearing it, honey." When he winked, I felt butterflies flutter in my stomach.

"Come on you two," Jackie called, waving us over. "Everything's on the table, and we're ready to eat."

Phil untied his grill apron and tossed it onto a lawn chair. He set the tray of burgers in the middle of my specially hand-built picnic table that seated twelve. It was so long and heavy, it would probably never leave my backyard. He and I took our seats and the passing of dishes began. The usual summer fare awaited us: Phil's pure beef burgers, fried chicken, potato salad, cole slaw, deviled eggs, chips, baked beans, lemonade and cold beer. It was a day for celebration.

As everyone dug in, I gazed around at the women I'd called friends my entire life. This time last year, we'd gone through an experience that bonded us even closer, if that was possible. This summer, I wondered at the way life had changed for us.

Last night we'd all attended the opening reception of Donna's first one-woman art exhibit. Since returning home from the National Parks Wonders Tour, she'd spent the last year refocusing her energy on something positive, rather than Chad's death and the money lost in Keith's financial scam. All her hard work and determination paid off. She'd sold six paintings of wildlife animals at the reception and had also been approached by the CEO of a prominent business to create a magnificent one-of-a-kind mural for their lobby.

As if that wasn't wonderful enough, she recently signed a contract to design a line of greeting cards with a wildlife motif for a major card company. Her future prospects were excellent, and she was talking of quitting her job as office secretary for the high school.

I popped one of Crystal's yummy deviled eggs into my mouth and watched her peel the crispy skin off her piece of fried chicken. The first thing she did when we returned from the west was to start an exercise program and begin to eat more sensibly, resulting in a ten-pound weight loss. In my eyes, she was perfect at any size, but Crystal was proud of her accomplishment, which made me happy for her. Shortly after losing the weight, she surprised us all by signing up with an internet dating service. That's how she met her boyfriend, Jared. He was a widowed engineer, father to a grown daughter, and grandfather to two small grandchildren that Crystal adored. Remarkably, he lived only thirty miles away. She promptly fell in love with all of them, and I hoped wedding bells would ring for her again in the future.

I still chuckle when I recall what she'd written in her dating application when it asked her to list the qualities she looked for in a man. She'd supplied: (1) a job, (2) all his teeth, and (3) monogamous. Apparently, Jared had fit the bill. More importantly, he was a good man who treated Crystal like a princess.

My gaze shifted to Annette, who was even more beautiful now at fifty-one than she ever was as a teen competing in beauty pageants. As she'd hinted on our trip, she and Bruce didn't make it. It wasn't but two weeks after we'd gotten home that she initiated divorce proceedings. Bruce didn't fight it, which confirmed for her that it was the right decision.

Something completely unexpected relating to the divorce was her son's reaction and ultimate support. She'd worried that her and Bruce's separation might send Dustin further over the edge, but it seemed to do the opposite. In time, he found a job and then a girlfriend, and had finally moved out of Annette's house last week. But not before their relationship had been repaired, which made her happier than I'd seen her in years. Now she was truly an empty nester, and she appeared to be relishing in her new freedom as a single, independent woman ready for adventures.

"Could you please pass the potato salad?" Kim asked. The bowl was in front of me, so I scooped a spoonful onto my plate and then passed it down the line. "Thank you!" she said, as I returned her contented smile.

True to her word, she'd come home and immediately gone into counseling. It didn't take many sessions for her to discover that the shoplifting correlated with her issues of never marrying or having children. Lo and behold, those issues all related directly to Eddie. After ten years, she dumped him and kicked him out of her house.

The man who sat next to her now at our picnic was a guy we'd graduated from high school with. He'd had a few tricky issues of his own to deal with in the past, but had been clean and sober for three years, held a regular job, and had just enough of an edge to hold Kim's interest. Having always been a rebel, both of Eric's arms were decorated with tattoos, he wore a diamond stud in one ear, and I often saw her on the back of his motorcycle as they tooled around Harley's Grove. Although he looked tough, turns out he had a soft spot for cats and babies, which I found endearing.

They'd only been dating for several months, but we'd known Eric all our lives. When Kim confided in me a couple of weeks ago that she thought he was going to pop the question, I couldn't have been more thrilled. It was about time someone realized what a catch she was. Hopefully soon, she'd have that big wedding with red roses and gold accents that she'd dreamt of since she was a young girl.

Jackie's granddaughter woke from her nap fussing. "She looks like a little doll dressed in that pink and white polka dot outfit," I commented. Jackie lifted Tiffany from the car seat she'd been sleeping in on the grass.

"I think someone needs her diaper changed," she cooed, giving the baby a kiss on the forehead. After she'd put a fresh diaper on, she opened a jar of baby food and held Tiffany in her arms and fed her while her own food grew cold.

I couldn't have been more proud of my friend. The change in Jackie began the moment we arrived back in Harley's Grove. She told Chris Stevens to take a hike—as well as any other man who tried to hit on her. Her focus became her husband; helping to care for him and making his final days as comfortable as possible.

Milton died in August and, as promised, he left everything to her. No one came forward to challenge the will, so she was wealthy beyond her wildest imagination. Before Milt passed away, she told him how much she cared for him and appreciated all he'd done for her. It was unknown whether he understood, because he was heavily medicated those last couple of weeks. At the end, Jackie stayed by his bedside holding his hand and swears she felt a tiny squeeze right before he breathed his last breath.

In December, Tiffany was born. I'd never seen Jackie respond to someone with such unconditional love and devotion, and that included her own three children. As far as her kids went, she was determined to improve her relationships with all three and was making good strides. Since Madison and her husband were just starting out with their marriage and careers, they graciously accepted Jackie's offer to live in one wing of the mansion. Now she was able to see her daughter and granddaughter every day. They seemed to be all she needed.

When I asked her recently if she ever thought she'd marry again, her answer was an emphatic "Not on your life."

As for me, this confirmed bachelorette finally gave in. Upon my return from the west, Phil came over the night after I got home, handed me a dozen roses, and cooked me a fabulous steak dinner, which we ate by candlelight. Afterwards, we snuggled together on the couch listening to music. When the song ended, he told me he'd missed me something awful while I was away. Then he broke my cardinal rule. He told me he loved me. He said he didn't want to spend another day without me. I just about passed out when he presented me with a beautiful emerald-cut diamond ring and asked me to be his wife.

Realizing that I wanted to go to sleep with him every night and wake up with him every morning, I told him I loved him, too, and I'd be proud to marry him. He let out a whoop and took my face in his big hands and kissed me like I'd never been kissed before.

Our wedding will take place in October, right here in my backyard under the oak trees. Jackie, Donna, Crystal, Kim and Annette will stand beside me as I promise to love and cherish my man. But not obey, I joked when I showed them my ring.

The bond between the six of us is stronger than ever. Once we left Colorado that day, none of us heard from the Denver police again. Supposedly, Keith's death was ruled an accident. It's not something we ever talk about. On the flight home, we vowed to take the secret of that night in South Dakota to our graves.

Sometimes when I'm alone, the memories will

come rushing back, and I'll sit straight up in bed in a cold sweat. But as life goes on in Harley's Grove just as it has for 185 years, the nightmares come fewer and farther between.

The girls and I still meet in Crystal's garage every Monday night. Nowadays, we share a lot less complaints and more laughter. Recently, Kim mentioned it's about time we learned some new dance steps.

They used to look to me for things like that, but after fifty years, I've learned a new word: delegate. And it sure feels good to be down from off that pedestal. I never did like heights.

ABOUT THE AUTHOR

Stacey Coverstone is a multi-published author in a variety of genres: women's fiction, contemporary and historical western romance, mysteries and suspense, and ghost stories and Gothics. She lives in Maryland with her husband, their dogs and cats, and a paint horse named Bill. They have two grown daughters and a baby granddaughter. When she's not writing, Stacey enjoys reading, photography, target shooting, traveling, and making scrapbooks of her adventures.

To view all of Stacey's books with blurbs, please visit her website at: http://www.staceycoverstone.com.

If you'd like to be notified of new releases, feel free to subscribe to her announce only newsletter group. You won't receive any spam. You can also find all of her books in the Kindle Store.

If you enjoyed this story, please consider posting a review on Amazon.

Thank you!

Printed in Great Britain
by Amazon